GUARDING HIS
OBSESSION

TABLE OF CONTENTS

SNOW & MISTLETOE

CHAPTER ONE

ZOEY

"I don't need a bodyguard," I huff into the phone, holding it between my shoulder and ear as I dig through my messenger bag for my keys.

"This isn't up for debate," my own assistant snaps through the phone. Maybe having my older sister as my personal assistant wasn't the best idea. That's a lie and I know it. Hell, who am I kidding, she holds my life together. I might be the brains of this duo, but she's way more organized than I am. It probably has something to do with her modeling career and always having so many things going on in her life at one time. She'd done it from the age of seven all the way until her mid-twenties when she retired. Elle is the order to my chaos, and I need her.

Now that I think about it, I don't think I even hired her. She just barged in, in true Elle form, and took over. It wasn't like she needed the job. She saved her money and I, in turn, helped her invest it in ventures I knew would do well.

"Grr. Where are these stupid keys?" I mumble to myself, digging deeper into my seemingly bottomless bag.

"Front left pocket."

I roll my eyes, only because Elle isn't here to see it. I can hear the smug tone in her voice. I reach into the front left pocket and pull out my keys.

"It's creepy when you do that."

"No, what's creepy is the stalker who seems to only be getting worse." I hear the worry in her voice. I'd probably be the same way if this was directed at her. But a stalker for me just seems strange. If anyone should be stalked, it's her. Some of the letters she would get when her modeling career was in full swing went from weird— like wanting to shave off all their hair and send it to her—to crazy, men offering her the world if they married her. Even telling her they wouldn't make her sign a prenup. You should see the way men get all dreamy eyed around her. It's actually kind of funny. How they follow her around like lost puppies with no brain. I've seen firsthand the smartest of men go utterly dumb in her presence. I've worked with some of the most intelligent, gifted men in America, but when Elle would show up to drop something off for me, they'd go from brilliant to incapable of putting a sentence together.

I insert my key in the door, turn it, and the alarm to my condo starts to sound. I hit the disarm button on my keychain before dropping the keys back into my bag, not into my left front pocket. Just a little rebellion because Elle can't see me.

"Okay. I'll meet with someone." I give in easily because there really isn't much of a choice. Fighting Elle on something she wants is like fighting a brick wall. It's better to spend your energy elsewhere.

I flip the lock back in place and turn, hitting a concrete wall of a man.

"Good, he's already there," I hear Elle say as my eyes travel up and up an endless span of chest. Up, up, up, until my eyes finally land on a hard face with a clenched jaw.

I blow my hair out of my face, trying to get a better look at him. Jesus. He's hot in that oh-my-God-he-could-crush-me way. Wait, is that hot?

It's then I realize he has his hands locked on my shoulders, holding me in place. I likely would have landed on my ass as hard as I ran into him if he hadn't grabbed me. My body presses against his, and I watch his nostrils flare as he takes a deep breath, like he's breathing me in.

His arms release me, and one hand goes to the glasses on my face, fixing them.

"What's he made of? Concrete and sex?" I whisper into the phone like the man in front of me can't hear me. He has the words "Hart Security" on his chest. I watch as he takes two steps back from me.

"Is he hot?" my sister asks, seeming to have perked up at my words.

"*Hot* is putting it mildly."

The man in front of me narrows his eyes as they travel down my body. I'm short, with lots of curves, and for the first time in my life, I wonder if a man likes what he sees when looking at me. My sister always gets the male attention. This isn't new to me, nor does it bother me. It is what it is.

It's how it's always been. She's tall, blonde, and has the bluest eyes. She's also skinny as hell, even though she could out-eat me. I'm the complete opposite. Short, lots of curves, with brown hair and eyes. I tend to blend in. I actually enjoy this since I'm not the best conversationalist. I have this problem where I have no mouth-to-brain filter, and that seems to make others uncomfortable. I've seen Elle cringe on occasion from the things that have slipped out of my mouth. It doesn't bother me like it seems to everyone else, though.

Just like Mr. Sex here, who has already taken a few steps back from me.

"Wow. He's got to be amazing. I don't think I've ever heard you call someone hot."

My stomach flutters at her words. They ring true. No, I don't think I can ever recall a time when I thought a man was hot. Symmetrical, maybe, but he definitely isn't that. His nose looks like it's been broken a time or two and a small scar runs across his left cheek.

I wonder if he has more. I take a step towards him, wondering if he'll let me see. I have no idea why I have the need to know if he has more. It doesn't make sense. I always have a reason for doing things and thinking things.

"Do you have more scars? Can I see them?"

I hear his intake of breath, and then Elle bursts

into giggles.

"Did you just imply you wanted him to get naked?" Elle says through laughter.

The man in front of me clenches his fists, and I wonder if this is another one of those times I'm making someone uncomfortable again.

"I..." I pause to think about it for a second. I didn't think about him having to undress for me to see more of him, but now I like the idea. I lick my lips.

"Let me talk to him," Elle says, still giggling.

I clench the phone in my hand for a second before I pull it from my ear. I'm thankful she isn't here in person, and I instantly feel guilty for that thought. I love my sister, but the idea of her getting this man's attention, a man I don't even know, bothers me. That can't be normal.

I hit speakerphone and let her know she's good to go.

"Mr. Hart, it's Elle. We talked on the phone this morning. I just wanted to thank you again for taking the job personally and not handing it off to someone else. I'm told you're the best."

"Ms. Barber, the security here is shit. I got in past the alarms completely unnoticed. The doorman didn't even give me a second look." His eyes lock on mine again for the first time since I was plastered to his body. "Furthermore, your sister seems to have no fucking problem with a man she doesn't even know standing in her home."

The last bit comes out in a yell and makes my eyes widen.

"I'll call you back." I click the end button on the phone screen before narrowing my eyes at Mr. Hulkman over there. Where the Hulk turns green and gets all giant, this guy seems to go all red and appear even larger than his massive self.

"Listen here, Hulk. You can take your incredible body and vacate my home. I won't be needing your services."

My face warms a little at the word *services*.

He takes two steps towards me, crowding my space, a space he didn't seem to want any part of a little while ago. He lowers himself so we're nose to nose.

"Sorry, cupcake. Contract's signed. You're mine."

CHAPTER TWO

DRAKE

Leaning into her, I catch the smell of sweet sugar. She smells like cakes, and it makes my mouth water. I wonder if she tastes as good as she smells. I'm annoyed that I can't keep the thought out of my head as I try to concentrate on the situation.

Elle Barber sent an email to us early this week requesting security for her sister. I'd never heard of her, but apparently two of the guys that work for me had, and they let me know right away they would love to take over the case. My partner, Daniel Pinkoski aka Pink, was in the dark like me. But after one of guys Googled her for us, I think Pink may have swallowed his tongue. He hasn't said a damn word since he saw her picture, and I'm beginning to wonder if he's in shock.

Seeing Elle didn't do a thing for me. I was more

concerned about why she thought her sister needed security and not her. After all, Elle is the famous former model. I don't know why models have to be so skinny. Give me a big girl, thick with curves, and I'm a happy man. I want a woman with a little chunk to her. Something soft for me to cuddle against, not that I've ever cuddled a woman before. But maybe I'm just describing Zoey, because ever since I laid eyes on her picture, she's the only thing I've been able to see, and thoughts of her in my bed pulled at me as I ran my hands all over her.

Elle sent over a package of information including a picture of Zoey. The second I saw her, I knew this case wasn't for anyone but me. *Fucking gorgeous* was all I could think. It took me a good ten minutes of staring at her picture before I moved on to what else was in the file. Emails and screenshots of harassing texts, several complaints filed with the police department stating her apartment had been broken into but nothing was stolen, reports detailing accounts of stalker behavior but with no other witness to give further details.

What had me worried the most was the fear I could hear in Elle's voice when she told me about what was happening. She's scared for her sister, and I don't blame her. The stalker was being more aggressive. What first looked like a little online bulling that I thought might be linked to getting information on something Zoey was working on started to morph into an obsession for whoever was doing this. I've seen this before, and things like this never end well, but I'm not going to let that be the case here. I'll do whatever it takes to keep Zoey safe, and from what her sister said, it's going to be a fight to get Zoey on board with any plans I might have.

I was with the Dallas police department in investigations for five years before joining their SWAT team. After a drug raid one night, when I took a bullet to my knee, I was permanently off the force. I was able to get back about seventy-five percent of the use of my leg, but it wasn't enough to let me back on the team. So I started a security firm with some friends, and it's been doing great. The guys on the force send a lot of business my way, and we take on private cases when we can.

After I talked with Elle on the phone, I let her know I would personally handle the case and make sure that Zoey got the full treatment. She'd get live-in bodyguard protection until we caught the stalker. I wouldn't leave her side until there was closure on the situation. It wasn't enough to make sure it went away. I needed to make sure it never happened again. For some reason, just looking at her picture made me feel protective of her. The thought of anything happening to her made my blood run cold.

Luckily, I don't have anything keeping me from staying with Zoey for as long as it takes. I've always been kind of a loner. My dad skipped out on my mom and me when I was little, and my mom died two years ago from a heart attack. She drank like a fish and smoked like a chimney, but it was fast when she passed, thankfully. The only family I have now is my boy Pink, but he comes from a big German family that's always making him eat, and I try not to get up in his business. I know he just wants me to join in on their fun, but having never really had much of a family, I always feel awkward and don't know what to do with myself when I'm around them. It's better he just goes and does his family thing and we hang out after.

Getting into Zoey's apartment was a fucking joke. The doorman was asleep at the counter when I went by, only slightly stirring when the ding of the elevator went off. Getting into her apartment and bypassing the security was just as easy. The system isn't a bad one, but putting four zeros as your passcode isn't smart. For all this talk about this chick being a genius, she didn't seem to think that through.

"Cupcake? What does that mean?"

She doesn't flinch at my words. Instead, she tries to get closer to me. This chick looks way too innocent to be trying to pull one over on me. *What's her motive,* I wonder, narrowing my eyes at her.

"It means I'm here as your hired bodyguard, which also means I'm staying here. My name is Drake Hart, and I'm in charge of your security." I make my words firm, brooking no argument. Her sister said it might be hard to get Zoey to agree to the security, and normally I wouldn't take a case like that. I don't want to be chasing after someone who doesn't want our services, but with her, I've found myself making an exception. The need to make sure she is safe is riding me hard. I can't let someone hurt her It is clear she needs someone to watch over her and I am going to make sure that person is me. "Want to show me to your spare bedroom?"

"Aren't you going to sleep with me?" she says, tilting her head to the side, still looking up at me.

My cock got hard the second she walked in the door, but I swear to God, I just popped a button on my jeans. The damn thing is going to bust through any second if she keeps talking to me like this. Fuck, to be in her bed with her...I wonder if her sheets smell as good as she does.

Looking into her eyes, I see no seduction or hidden agenda. She genuinely thinks that I'm supposed to sleep with her. "And why would I do that?" I nearly choke out before taking a deep breath, trying to pull myself back.

"If you're here to protect me, day and night, the closest place to do that is by my side. You could show me your scars then."

She looks down my cheek and over my body unapologetically, and I'm once again stunned by her bold talk. What the fuck? How has this curvy goddess not got a ring on her finger? Following her forward lead, I go for it.

"Why aren't you married?"

"I've never found anyone I wanted to test intercourse with." Her words are simple and to the point. Almost like I should just know this.

Someone could come in and knock me over with a feather right now. Is this girl telling me she's untouched? Jesus Christ.

"You always this forward?" I ask to see what she says. Seems she likes the truth. No beating around things.

"I guess so. Most people hate it. I say what I

11

think. I think my mind works a bit different than most. I guess I'm sorry if I offended you. But I don't see how. I was just answering your questions."

I feel myself smile a little, and I let out a breath. "No. I like it. Cuts through the bullshit."

CHAPTER THREE

ZOEY

I just stare up at him as I debate my options. Everyone seems to think I need security, but I just can't seem to wrap my mind around someone stalking me.

"I'm not sure this is all necessary."

His dark green eyes narrow on me, the half-smile dropping from his face. Maybe he doesn't like me cutting through the bullshit as much as he thought.

"I'm standing in the middle of your apartment, and you didn't so much as scream. This is despite you knowing someone has been stalking you. I could have been that someone. Fuck. I could *be* that someone."

I snort and roll my eyes.

"Yeah right, Hulk-man." I pat him on the chest before resting my hand there. I start to rub. I only meant to do a quick pat, but now I can't seem to remove my hand. I like the feel of him. I don't think I've ever liked the feel of a man before. I don't think I've ever had the urge to touch one before.

Once I let some CEO of a company I was working with kiss me. It was slimy and awkward and I hadn't had the desire to try it again. I only did it that one time before because I wanted to see what it would be like to kiss. Why so many people always felt the need to do it.

"You think I couldn't hurt you?" He grabs my wrist, pulling it away from his chest. The action makes me frown. Oh, I know he could hurt me, but someone like him would never stalk me. That just didn't add up to me. If anything, I'd end up stalking him.

"Oh, I'm sure you could Hulk smash me." Now that I'm not touching him, I bring my other hand up to his chest and continue doing what I was doing before, but he just grabs that wrist, too.

"Then why aren't you worried?" His words are hard and laced with anger. So unlike the soft hold he has on my wrist. I could easily pull away with one good tug. Maybe.

"Someone like you wouldn't stalk me. Maybe my sister. In fact, I don't see anyone stalking me. There has to be a mix up."

He gives a little tug on my wrist, and I fall into him, gasping when I feel his erection press into me.

"You're hard." The words pop right out of my mouth like they always do. I push myself further into him, wanting to feel it more.

"Shit," he grunts before stepping back and

releasing me. He starts to pace back and forth, reminding me of a caged lion at the zoo wanting out. I've clearly made him uncomfortable, and for someone reason that makes *me* uncomfortable. Normally, I don't care what people think about the things that come out of my mouth.

"Maybe you should just guard my sister. I'm sure..." My words trail off when he stops prowling back and forth and his eyes lock on me.

"Already put someone on her."

"So you agree it's she who needs protecting?" I hate that I was right. For one, I don't like the idea of my sister being in danger and two, my mind keeps going back to him sticking to me like Frodo to the ring.

"No. I one hundred percent think someone wants you, and they'll use anything to get to you."

"I just don't get it." I shake my head.

"There isn't anything to get. Just let us do our job and we'll find the asshole. And we'll keep both of you safe in the meantime."

I drop my bag to the floor and take a deep breath. My mind seems to be going down an endless tunnel of whos and whys. I just can't seem to grasp at anything.

I feel a finger lift my chin and find myself looking at him. My glasses slide back on my nose. I didn't even hear him move towards me.

"I can protect both of you. Your sister, too. I know it will make you both feel better knowing you're safe. What can it hurt? You won't even notice I'm around."

ALEXA RILEY

"That's highly improbable. You're ginormous and look like a male sex god."

"You can't say shit like that to me." He runs a hand through his hair like I've made him uncomfortable. So much for cutting through the bullshit.

"Sorry. I—"

His mouth hits mine, cutting off my words. For a moment I'm still not sure what just happened. I thought I had pissed him off. I dig my fingers into his shirt as he continues to go at my mouth. When I feel his hands go to my ass, I gasp. He takes the opening and pushes his tongue into my mouth.

I let my eyes close as he devours my mouth. This is nothing like the kiss I had before. I push my tongue into his mouth, mimicking his movements, wondering if I'm making him feel what he's making me feel.

My body feels like I'm buzzing. Something inside of me is coming to life. I push further into him, wanting to be closer. I deepen the kiss. He goes to pull back, but I wrap my hands around his neck, not even noticing that I'm eye level with him and that my feet are no longer on the floor as I pull him back to me.

I move against him, needing the friction. His cock is settled against my core, and I move my hips against him, taking what I want. What I need. Everything else is forgotten, my mind just shuts off.

He growls into my mouth, and I swear the sound vibrates through my whole body and goes straight to where I need it. My body explodes. A moan falls from my lips as I finally pull them from his. I let my head drop back and enjoy the sensations rocking through my whole body. I feel like I'm floating.

When I finally come back down, I realize I kind of am. My legs are wrapped around his waist and I've somehow ended up with my back to a wall. I feel his tongue come out and lick my neck, making my body jerk.

"I wanna do that again," I say lazily. I think I could do that over and over again.

"Your place isn't secure. Come to mine and I'll do it over and over again."

"Mmkay," is all I say. I'd probably go anywhere he asked me at the moment.

"Holy shit."

I roll my head to the side and see my sister standing in the doorway. A man stands beside her with a shocked looked on his face, mirroring Elle's expression. I'm guessing that's her guard.

"I'm keeping this one," I say, locking my arms around him, not wanting to do a trade.

"Fuck," Hart says, placing me on the floor. I regretfully let my arms fall from around his neck.

He steps in front of me, blocking my view of my sister and the other man.

"I don't think you should be her guard, Hart," I hear the other man say. His words make my heart drop.

"I'm moving in with him," I retort, popping my head out from behind him. Elle giggles. Both men just ignore us.

"Fuck," Hart says again, like it's the only word he

knows at the moment. He runs his hands through his hair again. It must be something he does when he's frustrated.

"We can get Kent to guard her," the other man says, making me scowl at him.

"No," Hart bites back, finally giving us another word besides *fuck*. "I'll get it under control," he says before looking down at me. "Go pack your stuff."

CHAPTER FOUR

DRAKE

How did I not hear anyone sneak up on us? I'm kicking myself for being so lost in our kiss that I didn't have any idea about what was happening around us.

Kiss. It sounds like such a small word for what just happened. Sweet Zoey rubbed her body against mine and got off on it. She used me for her pleasure, and fuck if it wasn't the hottest thing I've ever done in my life. Dry humping her against a wall is better than anything I've ever felt, and all I can think about is how fucking good it's going to be when I get inside her.

No.

I've got to distance myself. I can't get clouded again. Her protection needs to be my number one priority. When her lips hit mine, I was lost to everything around me. So far gone that I didn't notice my partner or Elle standing in the doorway.

What is happening to me? I've never been this gone over someone. The second I saw her picture I was a goner, and now, having tasted her sweet lips, I don't know that I can keep away from her. Which is probably why I should. She needs to be protected, and I obviously can't do that while I'm with her.

"Maybe you're right," I mumble as I watch Zoey walk out of the room.

"From what I saw, I think you've got it covered," Elle says. I look over and watch as she folds her arms across her chest and gives me a smirk. "I think most people would be offended to walk in and find this situation, but I've never seen her have this reaction to someone." She cocks her head to the side and smiles at me. "You must be quite the catch."

Pink lets out a low growl in his throat, and I look over to see an irritated look on his face. Elle seems to sense it, too. She looks over at him and a blush creeps across her cheeks.

"I think I'll go help my sister pack," she says, walking out of the room. I see Pink try to take a step towards her, but he holds himself back, staying in the front of the condo with me.

"What the hell happened?"

I turn to look at Pink, not knowing how to answer. Rubbing the back of my neck, I try to ease some of the tension there. How do I even begin to explain what is going on?

"I just... "I try to think of the right word, but nothing is coming.

"Reacted," he finishes for me, and it's the truth.

I never stopped to think about what I was doing or what the consequences would be. It was pure need and lust that drove me to her, against her. Inner raging desire beyond anything I've ever felt pushed me past the point of reason and sanity.

"Yes." The word leaves my lips like a curse.

"Do you need me to step in? Call someone else? I'll be honest, Hart. Looking at you now, I don't know anyone who would willingly cross you. You look like you're about to rip apart a truck."

Pink walks over and leans against the bar in the kitchen area. He tries to be smooth about it, but I can see he's moving his line of sight to the bedroom to watch the women back there. I know because I've been doing the same thing.

"I'll get it together. I don't want anyone else on this." I feel my fists clench. I know I can't handle the other option of having someone else this close to her.

"If it makes you feel any better, we kind of snuck in."

Pink smiles at me and gives me a wink. Bastard is almost as quiet as I am. He's probably the only person on the planet who could sneak up on me, so I don't feel as bad as I did before.

"You okay with staying with Elle? I'd like for both of us to remain on the premises or for them to stay with us until this is taken care of."

He gives me a quick hard look and nods. "I've got her taken care of."

"I set up video surveillance outside this building and inside the apartment. If the stalker tries to come back in, I'll know it."

"Good. I've got everything set up at Elle's place. I'm willing to give it a night or two there before I offer to move her. Since the threat wasn't directed at her, my being there might just be precautionary," Pink says, trying to look farther down the hall.

We wait quietly for a few more moments before Elle makes her way up the hall to us. "I think you might need to talk to Zoey about what the word 'essentials' really means." She gives me a wink and walks by us, heading for the front door. "You coming?" She turns to look at Pink, eyeing him up and down.

"God, I hope so," he whispers, loud enough for only me to hear, as he pushes away from the bar and makes his way to the front door with Elle.

I nod to the two of them before going to find Zoey. "I'll be checking in regularly with you both. No radio silence. No matter what. Clear?"

"Yes, sir," Pink answers as Elle gives a salute. They walk out of the door, her laughing and him rolling his eyes. I hate to say it, but he may have his hands full with that one.

Speaking of handfuls.

I have to stop that train of thought before I get to Zoey. I'm here to protect her, and I can't do that if I'm distracted. Maybe when we get to my place, I can jerk off in the bathroom real quick and take care of this ache. I'll just think about having her rub up against me and I'll be cumming in seconds.

I adjust my cock as I walk down the hall and into her bedroom.

I've already been in it before. I did a sweep when I first got into the apartment. It's much like the rest of her place. Bare walls, plain bedding, and nothing personal anywhere except for the picture of her and her sister beside the bed. Every room is extremely tidy, except for her office. Zoey is a minimalist with no knickknacks or clutter. But I had to laugh on entering her office. I'm sure she considers it organized chaos, but for someone who works online for ninety percent of her time, her office is really where she lives. Maybe if she ventured outside of it more, her house would reflect it the same chaos of her office, but as it is, her bed hardly looks slept in.

I see her over by the bed filling three huge suitcases to the brim.

"Cupcake, I don't mind you bringing a lot of stuff, but I think the Christmas tree can stay."

She pauses and looks up at me, a Christmas wreath in her hands. "Oh."

The sad look crosses her face, and I feel an ache in my chest. I'm by her side in seconds, holding her face in my hands as she drops the wreath to the floor.

"Don't make that face. I'm sorry. I just meant this was a quick trip to my house. You can bring anything you want. I can come back for all your stuff tomorrow or the next day. I just needed you to pack an overnight bag now."

She smiles really big, immediately over the sadness, understanding what I mean. I have to remind myself that she takes everything in the most literal sense.

"Okay. So just a couple of things. I can do that."

"Perfect."

I help her pack a couple of changes of clothes, and I grab her bathroom stuff before we go into her office to see what she needs from there. She packs up her laptop and one more bag filled with files. I have no idea what these are, but they seem important enough for her to bring. I'll ask her about them later. Right now I'm focusing on keeping her safe, and that means getting her out of here and to my place. There's no place safer than where I live.

"Okay, big guy. I think I'm ready."

I look down and try not to laugh. She's still holding the Christmas wreath under her arm, but I don't dare say a word. If she wants to bring her whole goddamn house, she can. It seems odd and out of the ordinary, but I find her quirkiness adorable, and her honest approach to this is refreshing. I think most people would be terrified of a stalker, but Zoey seems to take it in her stride.

"After you, cupcake."

To my surprise, she reaches out and squeezes my ass as she walks by.

"Just wondering what it felt like. Okay, let's go."

Smiling and shaking my head, I grab her bags. This is going to be interesting, to say the least.

CHAPTER FIVE

ZOEY

"Wow, I love this place." I look around Drake's home in awe. Everything is awash in deep, rich colors, making it feel warm and homey, nothing like my apartment.

"Thanks." I look up at him and see a little pink hit his cheeks. God, he's so handsome. My eyes go back to the scar on his cheek. I can't seem to keep my eyes off it. I couldn't stop staring at him the whole drive over here. I have no idea what it is about him, but for the first time in my life, I'm utterly fascinated by a man. He makes me feel things I've never felt before, and I like those feelings. Want to keep them. They make me feel more like everyone else. Maybe it was the mind-blowing orgasm he gave me. They're something I'm going to be getting more of.

"It feels like a home. Mine is kind of…" I

scrunch my nose as I try to think of a word. "Cold."

"I wanted it to be homey," he says, using my own word. I can tell there's more there. That he has put a lot of effort into making his place feel warm and welcoming. It seems important to him.

"Are you sure you want me to live here with you? I'll destroy this place." I drop the bag from my shoulder, and when it hits the floor, I hear a few things spill out, making my words ring true. "I'm kind of a mess. That's why I try not to have a lot of things. Simple seems to work best for me."

The corner of his mouth quirks at my words. "I don't think anything about you is simple. And I think I can handle you." He looks down at me, his eyes roaming over me. I don't think we're talking about handling the same things.

I try to clarify. "I'm serious! My sister is a neat freak. She won't even live with me and she loves me. When I moved out on my own, I made sure I didn't have too much stuff and tried to just contain things to my office and bedroom—places I could close the door to if people came over."

I look around his place and see not only does everything look all warm and cozy, it looks neat. I've been here two seconds and I've already made a mess.

"I kind of like the idea of seeing your stuff all over my place." He bends down and picks up the bag I dropped, repacking the items that spilled out.

"That doesn't even make sense." He likes the idea of me going all Tasmanian devil in his place?

"Come on, I'll show you to your room."

He starts to head down a hallway, and I follow

him, trying to take everything in. "I'm staying in your room, right?"

I stop moving when I collide into his back. I was too busy looking around at his home to pay attention to where I was walking.

"I have to protect you, cupcake. I'm not sure how well I can do that with you in my bed."

"But I'm moving in, and you said you would give me more orgasms," I protest, not understanding. It makes sense if we sleep together. I may be new at this sex stuff, but I'm pretty sure most of it goes down at night. In bed. I hope we don't have to wait for the sun to go down because I kind want to do it now if it's anything like what he did to me against the wall.

"Moving in." He says the words like he doesn't understand them.

"I thought you said I was staying with you. That you'd send someone to get the rest of my things. I'll have to see about breaking my lease, but I'm sure it can be done for the right amount of money. And Elle says I have money coming out my ass so no worries there." Elle handles my accounts. I don't pay attention to money. I know how to invest well but I don't really watch the bottom dollar. I guess because I haven't really had to. When people reach out for my services, she always handles costs and payments. I just slide my Amex when I need something and the thing always works. Elle says I spend hardly anything, and I'll never burn through the money at this rate.

He just continues to stare down at me, his face completely unreadable, not that I'm good at reading people. Computer code, yes. People, I'm a total bust at.

I start to get uneasy.

"Don't you want to do that with me anymore?" Maybe he changed his mind. Elle does that all the time. One date and maybe a kiss on the cheek and the guy is left on the other side of the door. It got so bad she just stopped dating altogether. Maybe he was one orgasm and done.

Then it hits me. He saw my sister. I wasn't even paying attention. Most men lose it when they see my sister. I was so caught up in my orgasm haze and making sure I was moving in with him, I didn't even pay attention to his reaction.

"Do you want my sister now?" I blurt out. This is the first time I wish I could pull the words back because I'm not sure I want the answer.

"My cock is still fucking rock hard from when you dry humped me, and I feel like I might explode if I don't get the taste of you back in my mouth. I feel like a goddamn junkie needing a fix."

I throw myself at him, and he drops everything in his hands to catch me. I go straight for his mouth, latching myself to him, wanting to give him what we both need.

This time I push my tongue into his mouth, going at him like he went at me in my condo. I want a replay of before. He said he needed another taste, and I'm more than willing to give him one, but he pulls back entirely too quickly.

"You said you've never had sex," he says, studying my face.

"I haven't." I run a finger down the scar on his

face before I lean in and lick it. His body goes completely still.

"I don't know why I did that," I confess. "I keep thinking about the other ones you might have. Wanting to do that to them, too." This pull I feel to him is crazy. I can't seem to think about anything else. Gone is the workload I need to get done, the files and dates long gone and forgotten. My mind isn't seeing reason anymore. Just want. This has to be just like Frodo felt with that ring. Drake is all I can think about now, all that seems to matter.

"You're going to be the death of me." His words sound pained.

"Isn't it your job to keep people alive?"

He takes a deep breath, then pulls me from him. My feet find themselves back on solid ground, having been wrapped around his waist only moments ago.

"Yeah, that's the problem. I can't seem to pay attention to what's happening around me when you touch me and say the shit you do."

"Is that abnormal for you?"

"Fuck yes."

"I seem to be having the same problem." My shoulders drop. "Maybe your friend was right. It might be best if someone else guards me."

His hand comes under my chin, making me look up at him.

"I should. I really fucking should. I'm being selfish doing it on my own, but I can't. I want you here."

"I want to be here, too."

He releases a breath and nods. "I need to look

into some more stuff about who's stalking you. If you can stay here in my home, I'll know you're safe. I just need to get my head on straight. I'll show you to the room and I'll be back in a few hours."

"Which room?" I press, biting my lip as I try not to smile.

He groans and runs a hand over his face.

"My room."

"Isn't it ours if I live here now?" I say simply.

"How come the things that come out of your mouth, the things that should have me running the other way, just get me fucking harder?" He reaches down and adjusts himself, and my eyes go to his cock. The same cock that I want to rub up against like in my apartment.

I ignore his question because I don't get what he means.

"Can we do that thing again before you go?"

"How are you a virgin with a mouth like yours?"

"Because I haven't ever asked someone to make me orgasm before?" I try to run through my mind, thinking if there was ever anyone that I would have wanted to have intercourse with but I just hadn't asked.

"What are you thinking about? I see your mind working." His hand comes to the middle of my brow, and he rubs me there, like he's trying to push the wrinkles out. Elle always says I scowl when I'm thinking really hard.

"I'm trying to think if there's someone else I could have had sex with."

Instantly I'm off the ground and over his

shoulder.

"Jesus, Hulk."

Before I can get my bearings, I'm flat on a bed with one very angry-looking man looming over me.

CHAPTER SIX

DRAKE

I move between her legs and look down at her surprised smile.

"I can't stand the thought of you with another man. I don't even want those ideas to cross your mind." Leaning in, I gently graze my teeth across her neck, feeling her pulse on my tongue. "I'm selfish. I want all of you, even your thoughts."

"Oh, that feels good. And don't worry. You're the only one I came up with when I thought about it."

I can't help but smile against her skin. The way she talks makes me feel like I can be completely open and honest with her. Like there's nothing she wouldn't want me to tell her, or her to tell me.

"Good."

I move between her thighs a little more, pressing

some of my weight down onto her. My hard cock rubs against her heat, and a shiver runs down my spine.

"Are you going to give me an orgasm now?"

I kiss up her neck and lick the shell of her ear, whispering, "Yes."

I pull back from her and reach down to unbutton her jeans, slowly pulling them down her hips. When Zoey reaches for her panties, I gently lay my hands on top of hers and look into her eyes. I shake my head slightly, letting her know to stop.

"Let's keep these on right now, cupcake. I'm only so strong."

She smiles up at me, her rich brown hair spread out across my pillow, and shrugs her shoulder. "You're the boss. Just so long as I get my orgasm."

I close my eyes, thinking about how much I want to sink inside her, but I clench my jaw and keep my restraint. Not yet. Just some petting, and that's it for now. I've got to keep my head on straight, and I know once I get inside her, there won't be any stopping me.

Once I've got her jeans off, I look down and see she's wearing just a T-shirt with a pair of pink cotton panties. My eyes zone in on her underwear, and I see a small wet spot. It's either from earlier or from now, but either way I lick my lips, wanting to taste it.

Reaching down to my own jeans, I unbutton the top button and unzip them. Pulling back the flaps, I expose my boxer briefs, straining from the massive erection behind them. I'm so fucking hard that this will probably be over in seconds. The tease from before nearly made me cum all over myself.

I know if I put my mouth on her pussy, I'll need to fuck her, so instead I lean forward, pressing our bodies together with only our underwear separating us. Our heat connects, and it's like lightning through my body. Her warm, wet panties brand the hard ridge of my cock.

I hump against her slowly, mimicking how I want to thrust into her. Her moans start to fill the room, and I look up to see her eyes closed and a big smile on her lips. Her arms are up grabbing the headboard as I pretend to fuck her.

Looking down to where I'm moving against her, I see the tip of my cock peek out of the waistband of my boxer briefs on every upstroke. He wants to come out and rub on her, skin to skin, but it's too risky. If I get my cock out, I'll want to push into her, even if she still has her panties on. Then I'll want to move them to the side and have her pussy kiss the tip. Then it won't be enough. I'll want all ten inches buried deep in her sweetness, and I need to hold back on that. I need to just do this and make this be enough.

With every thrust up, I feel her pussy dampen her panties further, and her moans get louder. I see the tip of my cock peek out again, and this time a thick drop of cum comes out and lands on her lower belly. I look at the sticky pearl there on her body, and suddenly I see her finger come down to touch it.

I follow her hand as she wipes it up and then brings her finger to her mouth. When she closes her lips around it and then hums in delight as she closes her eyes, I nearly cum all over her belly. The innocent act is so fucking erotic, I can hardly keep my body from shaking.

"That tastes nice. Maybe sometimes you could let me lick you there."

"Okay," is all I'm able to grunt out. I thrust hard against her pussy, feeling aggressive in my need for her.

I move my hips a bit lower so that when I thrust up, the tip of my cock bumps against her panty-covered clit. A couple of strokes leave a little white spot there from my cum. Every time my tip bumps her there, she moans louder. I can't help but try to give her what she wants, so I hold my uncovered tip on her clit and just softly pulse against it.

"More," she moans, closing her eyes and gripping the headboard.

I know where this will lead. I know what will happen if I give her more of what she's asking for. But I'm weak when it comes to her, and I give her more.

My fingers are shaky as I gently pull her panties to the side, exposing her bare pussy to me. She's got only a small amount of hair on her; it looks nearly naked. Her lips are puffy and soaked with need, and her clit is hard and begging for attention.

I press my tip to her clit, warmth and wetness welcoming it. It's all I can do to keep from clenching my eyes closed from the pleasure. I don't want to miss a second of it.

Rubbing my tip back and forth across her clit, Zoey moans louder as I leave small traces of cum on her. Her hips start to rise, like she's inviting me inside her, and I go stone still. I can't go inside her, not yet.

But her pussy is moving up and down, and she's trying to take me inside her.

"Fuck, Zoey."

"I think that would be nice." She moans and moves her hips up again, trying to make me penetrate her.

Taking my thumb to her clit, I rub her there a little and bring my thumb to my mouth. I need a little taste of her to help me keep my strength.

Her flavor hits my mouth, and I swear I feel a groan come out. It's too much, but it's not enough. I've got to get her off so I can cum and try to ease the beast I feel inside me.

Grabbing my cock, I go back to rubbing the tip of my cock on her clit. "Just like this, Zoey. Cum for me like this, cupcake."

I hold her hips down with my free hand, keeping her from trying to take my cock inside her. She wants more, but right now I'm only giving her what she needs.

I feel her pussy start to pulse as her back bows off the bed. She shouts my name, and the sound of it is enough to set me off.

"Drake!"

I watch as her body tenses and rides out the waves of her orgasm, and I cum all over her sweet little pussy. Thick jets of cum splash onto her clit, and I watch as I mark her. I move down a little, pressing the tip of my cock to her virgin opening, and release a little of my cum there, too. I don't know what possesses me to do it, but I feel like I have to shoot some in there, too. I want all of her to belong to me, even if I haven't fully taken her yet.

When the last of my cum has left my body, I grab Zoey by the waist and roll her over on top of me before I collapse all of my weight onto her.

I feel like I've been hit by a truck. My orgasm rocked me hard.

Suddenly, I feel Zoey sit up, and I open my eyes to see the biggest smile shining down at me.

"That was incredible. Now this time, I think I want to be on top so I can do what I want."

My still-hard cock pulses at the idea, but I shake my head as I smile back at her. "I'm beginning to think you only want me for one thing, Zoey."

She looks like she's contemplating something, and I try to shake her off her train of thought before she can tell me that maybe sex is the only reason she's interested in me.

"Let me show you my culinary expertise while we go over the stalker information. Deal?"

She leans down, gives me a quick kiss, and hops off my body. "Deal," she says, and she covers her cum-covered pussy back up with her panties and slides her jeans back on.

Why does the thought of me coating her make me impossibly hard all over again?

CHAPTER SEVEN

ZOEY

I watch him as he moves about the kitchen while I sit at the breakfast bar. His shirt is off, and I can see the ridges and lines of his muscles as he moves around. For such a big guy, he moves almost with a silent grace. I wonder if that has to do with his job. Something he was trained to do.

I've never been so fascinated with a man in my life, and the more I seem to learn about him, the worse it becomes. I can't seem to pull my eyes away from him, memorizing every mark on his body. At first I was intrigued by the scars that littered his body, but now my eyes linger on the tattoos that run up and cover every inch of both his arms.

"Do you like pain?" The question pops out of my mouth.

He turns to look at me, his back muscles flexing

once again. I wonder how much he has to work out to keep those things. I bet a lot. I know he can lift me like I weigh nothing at all.

"I wouldn't say I liked it. Why?"

"I don't know. Just all the tattoos and scars. Seems like you have lot of pain going on."

His head cocks to the side, a half-smile pulling at his mouth. At this angle I can see a dimple in his cheek, one I hadn't noticed before. Maybe because of his light facial hair, but I see it now.

"Scars kind of come with the job, and the tattoos kind of do, too."

"You have to get tattoos to be a bodyguard?" Maybe this is some kind of ritual they do. Like when my sister was a cheerleader and she wore ribbons in her hair and painted crap on her face. I didn't get it, but they all did it. It looked pretty stupid, but the tats don't look stupid on Drake.

He lets out a bark of laughter as he goes back to chopping up an onion.

"No, cupcake. It's not required. It just something the guys and I liked to do. I haven't gotten a new one in a long time."

"Do you want more?"

"Hadn't really thought about it. I think the last time I got one, I was with SWAT."

"You should get one with color."

He sets the knife down and runs a hand up his other arm, looking down at his tattoos.

"You don't like all the black?" he asks like he really cares. Elle hasn't asked me anything about fashion or what looks good in forever. I have absolutely no fashion sense, and mostly I just don't care. I just throw stuff on.

"Thought it might look nice." Everything about him seems dark and big. Almost scary. I really noticed it when I was studying him moving in the kitchen. He's right. I should have been scared when I walked into my apartment and he was just standing there. He's built like a freaking giant. His dark eyes and dark hair feed into the deadly edge. I'm sure he could just snap someone in half if he needed to. The tattoos and scars only add to his whole "I could snap you in half or go Hulk smash on you" mystique.

But when I first saw him, I knew something about him just felt right. I felt a pull to him like nothing I've ever known before. Heck, I am doing things with him I've never even thought about doing with anyone before.

"And what would you suggest?" he asks, like he'd actually do whatever it is I'd suggest.

"A cupcake?" I half-joke, thinking he'd never do that. "It could go right next to that skull."

Drake throws back his head and laughs. It rocks his body and makes me smile. I seem to even like him doing that, too. Everything he does gets me worked up. It makes me want to be wrapped around him again.

"I'm glad I'm moving in. I think I'll keep you. We seem to work better than I do with most people," I confirm. Yes. That seems logical. I could watch him all the time. Though I'm not sure how much work I'll get done. When I sat down at the breakfast bar, I'd intended to work on my laptop a little. I have a project that I need to get wrapped up—a big one—but my eyes couldn't seem to leave him.

"You keep saying 'move in here' like it's permanent. Is that what you're meaning, or am I not understanding you?"

"Is that not…" I pause, trying to think back to what he said. Something about staying with him and I'd be safe. He'd be my bodyguard while he found out who was stalking me. I drop my eyes away from him, feeling embarrassed. It's a feeling I'm not used to. "You just meant until you find out who's stalking me."

I can't bring myself to look up at him. Is this what all those guys feel like when Elle tells them to hit the road? I suddenly feel bad for them.

I sense him before he even touches me, standing by my side. Then he cups my face in his hand, making me look up at him. Even with me sitting in the high-top chair, he's still ridiculously taller than me. He bends down a little, bringing our faces closer.

"You can stay here as long as you like." He moves in a little closer. "I work better with you than I do with most people, too."

"Really?" I wiggle forward a little bit, wanting to be closer to him. My ass is practically hanging off the chair.

In one movement, he picks me up, takes my seat, and puts me onto his lap. My body straddles his thick thighs, and I settle against him perfectly.

"Yeah, really." He uses one hand to brush a strand of hair out of my face. "When your sister came to me about you and I saw your picture, I knew I'd be the one to take your case personally. I don't do personal bodyguarding anymore. I have men for that."

"Did you see a picture of my sister, too?" I ask, wanting to know. If Elle were here, she would have given me one of her elbow nudges to let me know it was a question I shouldn't be asking. Nine times out of ten, I know when I'm saying something I shouldn't. I'm not stupid, but subtlety just isn't a skill I could ever get myself to pick up. If I had a question, I asked it or found a way to get the answer.

"I saw hers first."

"And?" I nudge.

"And what?" His eyebrows come together like he doesn't understand what I'm getting at.

"You didn't want to guard her?"

"Like I told you, I put a guard on her." He grips my hips in a firm hold. "*I'm* guarding you. I didn't want anyone on you but me. From the first moment I saw that picture of you. Something hit me, and I had to see what it was. Call it the cop in me. Maybe it's the sixth sense you develop working on cases and busting down doors."

I wiggle a little in his lap.

"We do fit together well," I confirm.

"I can't think when you do that shit."

"I know. Isn't it amazing? It's like my brain shuts down for once. I always feel like it's going, but with you..." I pause, because I can't seem to think how to finish that thought.

"It's like nothing else matters." He finishes it.

"You feel it, too?"

"Yeah." He nods, resting his forehead against mine.

"I have no idea what I'm doing. I've never done this. Heck, it's always just my sister and me. I don't even really have any friends unless you count the ones I have on the internet. And most of the time, we're just in competition for stuff. I've never had a boyfriend. That's what you'd be, right?"

"Me neither."

I pull back to look at him. For once, he has to look up at me.

"Had a girlfriend," he finishes, and I just stare at him. I may not be into checking out men, but I know what women go for at least, and he fits the bill.

"But you're," I place my hands on his chest, feeling the tickle of his chest hair on my fingers, "you know, all sexy and stuff." I feel my face warm a little at the admission. Again, the embarrassment hits me, reminding me how he's so different to other men I've met.

"Let just say I'm not a real people person either. Never had the desire to have a girlfriend."

"But I'm right?" I edge, because he still hasn't confirmed this.

"That right there," his hands slide up my hips and back down, "and a few other reasons. That's why I'm so drawn to you. At first it was your picture, but from the moment you opened that mouth and things started to fall out, I knew I was fucked."

"I like when you say stuff like that. Makes me feel all warm inside." I slide my own hands up his chest and around his neck.

"Isn't that what boyfriends are supposed to do? Make their woman feel all warm inside?" He doesn't let me answer. He just leans in and takes my mouth in a kiss. This time it's soft and sweet, not like the ones we've had before. Almost like a conformation that he's mine now.

I feel bold, and I want to explore as much about this new sexual awakening as possible. Do all the things that girlfriends do.

I slide off the stool and push Drake's thighs apart.

"Cupcake." There's a dark edge to his voice, but I look up at him with a bright smile.

"I want to do girlfriend things."

I kneel in front of him so his cock is at eye level. I run my hands up his thighs, then reach into the waistband of his loose shorts and tug at them.

"I-" He starts to say something, but when I pull at his shorts again, he stops to help me slide them off. "I don't know if I can control myself," he grits out.

"I've never done this before, so it may not go so well. Just let me explore."

His giant cock bobs in front of me, and I lick my lips. I go to take off my glasses, but he stops me.

"Leave them on." His voice is filled with so much desire, it sends goose bumps across my body. It's so exciting that I've made him feel that way.

I feel his fingers in my hair as he brushes it out of my face, holding it back for me as I lean forward and open my mouth.

His warm flavor hits my tongue, and I moan around the head of his cock. He's a little salty, but I like the feel of him. His thighs tremble under my touch as I suck more of him into my mouth. He lets out a sharp breath, and more of his flavor floods my tongue.

I think he likes when I suck him, because the further down I go and swallow around his cock, the more cum seeps out. I start moving my mouth up and down, trying to suck at the same time to get more. I want to feel him cum in my mouth, and this seems to be the way to do it.

"Hands, Zoey," he grunts, and it sounds like he's holding his breath.

I bring my hands up to his cock, one goes to the shaft and the other to his balls. He's so hard, yet his skin is so warm and soft. The delicate ridge against my tongue feels sexy. I move the hand on his shaft in time with my mouth, and he immediately responds to that, giving me more cum, growling as he does so. I lightly massage his balls with my other hand, feeling them draw up as a few more drops of cum hit my mouth.

"Fuck. I can't last." His hands tighten in my hair, and he goes to pull me off of him. "Zoey, come off, baby. I'll cum in your mouth if you don't."

He tugs at my hair again, but I just grip him tighter and suck him deeper, not letting him take his cock away. I want him to lose control like I did with him.

"Goddamn, baby. I'm cumming."

His thighs lock up as his cum hits the back of my throat. I drink it down, sucking all of him up and making sure I don't spill any. He's moaning so loudly, and I love the sound. I love that I was able to do that to him. I feel so powerful at being able to get him off, and it's nice to know I can return the pleasure to him in some way.

When he's finished cumming, I take my mouth off his hard cock and give it one last kiss on the tip. He jerks in response, and I smile up at him, seeing his eyes are half-closed.

"I think I saw stars," he says, and it makes me smile.

"That was good?" I ask as he pulls me into his lap. I like that I pleased him.

"There's not a word to describe it. So much better than *good*, cupcake. Perfect." He grabs the back of my head, pulling me in for a soft kiss that I hate to pull away from.

"I think the food is burning." I know he seems to hate that I can distract him like that, but I love that I can do to him what he does to me.

"Shit." He jumps up and places me back on my chair before rushing over to the stove. He pulls a pan off and mumbles something about a *distraction*.

CHAPTER EIGHT

DRAKE

When I finish cleaning up after our meal, I go to the bar and put Zoey back in my lap. I had to recook everything, but I didn't mind because it gave me a chance to watch her work as she watched me cook.

"Tell me what you're working on," I say, leaning in and kissing her neck.

"I do data research for a couple of firms in and out of the country, oh, God, that feels good. Right there."

I smile against her skin "What was that?"

"Your mouth is very distracting. Don't stop. I'll keep talking."

I continue to kiss her as she wraps her arms and legs around me.

"Essentially, I collect financial information on people. Sometimes I'm hired by the government, and sometimes I'm hired by bad guys."

I tense at her usage of the term "bad guys." "What do you mean by that?"

"It's nothing really. I just take on cases I like. If I find something interesting, I do that."

She says it so nonchalantly. I'm not sure she understands the dangers of working for criminals when it comes to money.

"Cupcake, don't you think this could have something to do with your stalker now?"

She looks at me and cocks her head to the side as if contemplating it.

"No. I'm careful."

Just as I'm about to open my mouth and ask her some more questions, I hear the alert go off on my phone. I jump up, taking Zoey with me as I go to the other side of the counter and grab it.

Before Zoey walked in on me, I set up some things in her apartment. Hidden cameras, motion sensors, the works. If someone entered the apartment, I could monitor it. I had the alert set up on my phone.

I carry Zoey over to my laptop and set her down on the counter beside it. I open it up, put in my passcode, and wait a second for all the security cameras to come up to speed.

"That's my home," she says, leaning over and watching with me.

"Yes. It looks like someone got inside. The front door was opened, but there's no sign of forced entry." I zoom in on the image and see that the door knob and locks don't look damaged. I double-check the keypad system on my phone and see that the correct code was entered. "Whoever did this had a key and code."

"That's impossible. Only Elle and I have that."

I switch through cameras around the house, but I can't find any movement. I can't figure it out. Someone opened her door and turned off the alarm. I have a motion sensor going off at the entrance but nowhere else. Whoever was there must have seen something to scare them off.

I pull Zoey close to my side as I go through the camera footage. Finally, I get to the point when the sensors went off, and I see a dark shadow at the front door. The two of us lean closer to my laptop screen to try to make out the figure, but it's too dark and too grainy.

"Goddamn it," I curse, wishing I would have had more time to test out the equipment I put in place before we left. I was so concerned with getting Zoey here that I didn't test the sensors and cameras properly. "I'm sorry, Zoey. This is my fault."

"Why are you sorry? You're the one who got me out of there. I'm safe because of you."

I look into her eyes, and I see that she means it with all her heart. She's partly right. I did get her out of there before the person came back, but I can't help but feel a little guilty for not making sure we caught them at the same time.

"Do you recognize the person on the screen?" I have little hope she does. She would've told me already. With Zoey, I always know what's on her mind. And it's quite possibly my favorite thing about her.

"No. It's so fuzzy. It could be a man or a woman, and I can't even make out what they're wearing. It looks like they open the door, enter the code, and stand there for seven seconds before they turn around and leave. I don't think they even locked it behind them."

"That's an accurate description," I say, leaning over and kissing her cheek. "I'll pull the cameras from the lobby, but the system your building uses is less than adequate, and I'm not hopeful. It will take me some time to get the request back. They weren't very cooperative when I talked to them before. They said that unless a police report of harassment had been filed, they weren't required to tell us shit."

"Yeah, I'm really not a people person, but I should have done better research on the building security guys before I moved in. Some of them are alright, though."

"I'm sure they will work with us once I show them the footage of the break in, but I'm not sure how fast they'll work."

"So does that mean you have time to give me another orgasm before we'll have more information?"

I can't help but smile at her. I look back at my computer, sending the video along with an email to my team and her building requesting lobby footage. Once I click send, I turn to her, scoop her up, and carry her back to the bedroom.

"Yes. That's exactly what that means, cupcake. More orgasms. How many would you like?"

Leaning in, I bury my face in her neck, breathing

in her sweet smell as I go into the bedroom and get on the bed with her in my arms.

"All of them. And this time I want you inside me, too. I think it would feel magical."

I pull my face away from her neck and look into her eyes. "Zoey," I whisper. I'm not sure what to say. I want her so bad, and my cock is throbbing. But I worry it's too fast, and what happens when I get what I want and she tries to take it away from me? A panic comes over me, and I cling to her tightly. I can't let her leave me.

"I'm on the pill if you're worried about getting me pregnant. It helps regulate my periods. And I'm a virgin, so I don't have any sexually transmitted diseases. Do you?" She says it all so bluntly.

"No. I'm clean. It's been a really, really long time since I've done anything, and I've been tested since then. I just worry…"

I trail off, not knowing what to say. This conversation is usually the other way around, isn't it?

"What, Drake? What do you worry about?" She wiggles like she's trying to get closer to me, but we're already plastered together.

Letting out a deep breath, I look away from Zoey. "I just don't want you to use me for sex, okay? You mean something to me, and I'm afraid once I give in, you won't want me anymore."

When she doesn't answer, I look back into her eyes and continue. Cards on the table, right?

"I've been really shy around women my entire life, and I never know what to say, so I just don't say anything. I've only been with two women, and it was

ALEXA RILEY

once each time. I don't remember much about them
It was just a drunken mess to get it over with. I don't
have a lot of experience when it comes to this, but I
like that you tell me what you mean so I don't have to
guess. There are no games, and I know where I stand
with you. So please just tell me, for lack of a better
question, are your intentions with me honorable? Do
I have to worry about you being with me and then
sneaking out on me in the middle of the night? Will
we do this and then will you decide you don't want to
see where this goes? Because right now, I'll give you
all the orgasms you've ever wanted if you think I'm
what you want. But if you just want to play around
and have a good time, then maybe we should cool off
for a bit."

I feel exposed as I sit on the bed, holding Zoey to
me. This is probably the dumbest thing a guy has ever
done, trying to turn down sex for a relationship. But
there is something between us, something really
special, and I don't want to tarnish it by making light
of what I feel. And I don't want to be used as an
experiment because she's finally found a man she's
attracted to. I won't be able to let her go, but I'm
trying to keep my heart whole. In a very short time,
she's become important to me, and the thought of
belittling what is happening between us with a quick
decision makes me want to take a step back and really
find out what she wants from this.

CHAPTER NINE

ZOEY

I move to climb on top of Drake, and he easily lets me as he grips my hips in a firm hold as I straddle him. Resting my hands on his firm chest, I smile down at him. I'm not used to having someone touch me all the time, but I can't seem to get enough of him doing it. I like how his fingers always wrap around me like they've been doing it forever. It's something I'm going to enjoy now that I'll be living with him.

"I thought you said we're boyfriend and girlfriend. If that's not to your liking or solid enough, we can get married. That's what people do. Right?"

I feel the hands on my hips flex, and his dark eyes widen a little. I like that he seems lost in all of this, too. I was sure with the way he picked me up and handled me that he'd been with his share of women. Knowing that he hadn't warms me and makes butterflies take flight in the pit of my stomach. It's a feeling a man has never given me before. I like all of the feelings he's been giving me, and I want to keep them. The most logical thing to do would be to get married. That's what people do when they want to stay together. Then he would be mine. I lick my lips at the idea of him being only mine.

When he just keeps staring at me, I start to feel my heart sink. Maybe that was a little too far for him. Elle would tell me I'm moving too fast, like I do with most things. I never understand why people drag their feet with things. If you want something, you have to snatch it up or work towards getting it. I lack finesse, I'm often told, but I go after what I want.

"Zoey," he finally says, his voice soft, nearly a whisper. His body goes lax underneath me, but a pounding cuts off his words, and he pulls me from his lap and gets to his feet.

"Don't move." He shoots me a hard look, one I'm sure that works on a lot of people, but I've seen how fast I can get those eyes to change from hard to soft. They don't work on me like I'm sure he hoped they would. He pulls a gun out from his nightstand, and my eyes bulge in shock as he leaves the room.

I debate staying put, but it isn't much of an argument. I get off the bed quickly and peek out the door. Hearing voices, I slowly make my way down the hall to see Elle standing in the entryway, Pink right behind her with his hands resting on her hips like he's trying to keep her in place.

"Zoey!" She breaks free of Pink and runs towards me, wrapping me in her arms. "God, I'm so glad you agreed to do this. I saw the video. What if you'd been there? What if…"

Her words break off in a sob, and I squeeze her tighter.

"I'm fine. You don't have to worry. I'm with Drake. He'll keep me safe." She keeps crying, and I just whisper reassuring words to her until she finally pulls back, looking down at me, her eyes all red rimmed.

"Don't cry. You know that messes with me inside," I tell her before poking her, making her smile then sniffle.

"I'm staying here with you." She wipes her eyes before tucking her long blonde hair behind her ear.

"No," I hear Pink say as I look up to see him now standing right behind her, super close. I'd lost sight of both him and Drake when Elle crushed me in a hug. She might be thin, but she's tall, and still Pink towers over her. He might even have an inch on Drake, but where Pink is tall and lean, Drake is broad and solid.

I hold my breath, biting the inside of my cheek, wondering what's going to happen. People don't tell Elle no. Well, they can try, but it never works.

"Excuse me." She turns but bumps directly into him. I go to step back but find Drake there, and he pulls me into him, stepping back from both Elle and Pink.

"Don't even try it, *Prinzessin*. I got six sisters." He looks down at her with a smirk on his face, but his face softens and his hand comes out like he's trying to brush one of the tears from her eyes.

She bats his hand away, and the smirk just comes back to his face again.

"I'll do as I please," she replies tartly in the tone she uses when she's in her business, no-nonsense mode. The tears have disappeared, and her voice is clear as a bell.

"That so?" He takes a small step towards her, closing in any space between them. I can't seem to look away. It's like when you're playing a video game and only one man is still standing and the kill is at one percent. Only I'm not sure who is who in this situation.

"What's with you always being in my space? Just because you're guarding me doesn't mean you need to be up my ass."

"Can't blame me for wanting to get in there, *Prinzessin.*"

Elle pulls back her arm, and I close my eyes, not wanting to see the smack land. When the sound doesn't come, I crack one eye open to see Pink is kissing her. Not a soft kiss, but a full-on one I'm not sure I should be watching. The hand she had raised to him is now caught in his.

As if she realizes what she's doing, she pushes at his chest, and he easily steps back.

"I can't believe you!" She turns to look at me, her mouth all red. My hand goes to my mouth, and I wonder if I look like that, too. The thought makes that tingling feeling come back. Then her eyes go to Drake.

"These are the kind of people you hire at your security firm?" She half-yells at Drake, and I can tell she's flustered and unsure about what to do. It's a look I've never seen on her face before. Pink just stands behind her and shrugs like he's not worried about the hell Elle is about to release.

He clearly doesn't know about the time she and I went to Ben and Jerry's and they ran out of coffee ice cream. She got free ice cream twice a day for a month after that scene.

"Don't talk to my fiancé like that," I snap back at her, not liking that she thinks he's not doing his job right. I'm not sure what his job entails entirely, but he's been guarding me just fine. More than fine.

Elle's jaw drops open. Drake snags one arm around my waist, pulling me so my back is to his chest. I relax into his comfort, feeling his heat warm me up.

"Got you to stop crying," Pink says, the smirk now a full smile.

She whips her head back around, probably to give him a glare.

"Fuck, you look good riled up. I can't seem to help myself."

She turns back to me and releases a huff, and for a brief second I swear a small smile hits her mouth before she goes back to giving me the third degree.

"Fiancé? Don't you think that's a little quick, Zoey?" Her tone makes me want retreat because I know it all too well. It's the one I get when I'm not quite doing things right. Or what other people feel is right. Normal. I know she means well, but it still stings. Drake doesn't make me feel that way. He seems to get me. Even likes the things that just pop out of my mouth. Likes how fast I seem to rush into some things. As if reading my thoughts, he confirms that he doesn't think we're moving too fast either.

"No," Drake says, still holding me close. I turn a little to look up at him, and I know I've got to have a giant smile on my face.

"You can't stay here, *Prinzessin*. The new couple needs their alone time," Pink says to Elle.

I don't even turn to look at them. I just keep looking up a Drake who's got that soft look again.

"I told you to stay put," Drake whispers down to me.

"Sorry. I seem to like to follow you around," I admit to him, not caring if everyone can hear us.

"I like that, cupcake, but until I know you're safe, you gotta do what I tell you, or I'll worry nonstop. You'll do that for me?"

"Yes," I say instantly, wanting to give him what he wants.

"She never complies that easy with me," I hear Elle huff.

"Come home with me and I'll comply with anything you want."

"You're disgusting."

"You still wet from that kiss?"

"Zoey." Elle says my name, ignoring Pink's question.

I turn my head to look at her, and I notice she hasn't made a move to put space between herself and Pink.

"What?"

"I want to stay with you."

I shake my head. "I want to be alone with Drake. We have plans. Plans that involve me having lots of orgasms."

"His plans should be finding out who's stalking you." Elle stomps her foot in frustration, and I can't help but smile. Strangely, I like how this Pink guy has got her all worked up. Her calm and collected self is starting to slip away, being replaced by a looser, more natural Elle.

"He is. We'll just do that in between."

"She's right, cupcake. I do need to check in with the security at your building and see if they got those tapes." He leans down, placing a kiss on my neck. I lean up, giving him all of me, but he doesn't do the licking like I want and just pulls away. "You want to be close to Zoey? Stay with Pink. He lives one floor down, and the building is secure. You'll both be safe here."

"Fine."

I narrow my eyes at Elle. She gave in a little too easily.

"Call two guards. I want them on the door while we go check shit out," Drake tells Pink before turning to me.

"You and your sister keep your little asses planted while we're gone. When I get back, I'll give you what you want."

CHAPTER TEN

DRAKE

I hear Pink make the call as I take Zoey's face in my hands and gently kiss her lips. She opens for me, and I slip my tongue inside. As I taste her sweet warmth, I want to deepen the kiss and take her to the ground, but I hear a throat clearing and I remember we aren't alone.

"They'll be here in three minutes," Pink says as I pull back from Zoey's lips.

She's smiling so big that I can't help but match it. Leaning down, I give her one more quick kiss before I turn, going to the bedroom and pulling on some boots. Once I'm dressed, I head back out to the kitchen to see Zoey and Elle sitting at the counter and Pink standing on the other side, staring directly at Elle, nearly burning a hole into her.

"Everything okay?" He looks up at me, shaking

off the trance, and pushes away from the counter.

I hear a knock and check the security camera next to the door, seeing two of our men outside.

Nodding to Pink, I lean over and kiss Zoey on the forehead one last time. I can't seem to keep my hands off her, and even now, knowing she won't be in my sight makes me itchy to hurry this up and get back to her. It's a feeling I'm not used to, having always liked being alone.

Pink passes by me with a wicked look on his face. He walks over to where Elle is sitting, and before she can protest, he scoops her up out of her stool, dips her back dramatically like something from an old movie, and plants a kiss right on her lips.

I bite my lip to hold in the laugh, and I look at Zoey who is doing the same.

After a moment, he breaks the kiss, sets her back down on the stool, and walks away.

"Asshole," Elle mumbles as she touches her lips, and her cheeks turn bright red.

"As much as you keep mentioning your ass, *Prinzessin*, I can see that's going to need attention first," Pink says, not looking back as he walks out the door.

I look over to see Elle's mouth drop open and her cheeks burn even brighter, so I leave her and a laughing Zoey alone in the apartment. When we get outside, I talk to my guys posted outside as a precaution, then Pink and I head to my truck.

"You sure you want to keep digging that grave?" I ask, looking over as Pink gets in the truck.

"As long as I end up buried inside her, I'm

good."

He doesn't smile as he says it. The look on his face is serious. I just shake my head and start the truck, pulling out of the parking garage. I don't think I've ever seen Pink go at a woman like that before. He tends to be the one pushing them away. When I go over to his family's house for the holidays, his sisters' friends swarm him, and he's always, always trying to dodge them. It's new to watch him chasing one. Well, maybe *chasing* isn't the right word. It's more like he's *planted* himself.

"So you're engaged?" His question doesn't contain a trace of mockery. It comes out as an honest question, and I give him an honest answer.

"Yes."

There's not a second of hesitation in my answer. And not a single trace of doubt.

"Just like that?" he asks, and I hear the other questions that come along with that one.

"Yes," I answer, not ready to go into it with him. There's only one person I want to discuss this with and that's Zoey. It's nobody's business but hers and mine. She took me off guard so easily. She just threw getting married out there, and I'm not going to look a gift horse in the mouth.

I'm taking what she's giving me. Was it quick? Fuck yeah, but I don't care. We'll have the rest of our lives to sink into each other, and I just fucking know, gut instinct, that she's meant to be mine. And that instinct has kept me alive and has yet to steer me wrong. There's just something about her that fits me.

"Alright." Pink takes the hint, and I can hear a

little understanding in his voice as he pulls out his phone. "So what's the next move?"

"We head back to her apartment and talk to the security desk there. I didn't want to mention this in front of them, but my request for digital copies of their security feed was denied."

"Why? Didn't you explain the situation?"

I growl a little bit and think about the email I sent earlier requesting it. The email I got in response was a firm *no*. I thought a personal visit might help convince them.

When we pull up outside of Zoey's building, Pink and I jump out of the truck and go inside. The guard I spoke to earlier today is gone, and someone new is in his place.

The guy sitting behind the counter stands up as we approach. He's about our age—late twenties, early thirties—tall with dark hair and dark eyes. No tattoos or piercings. His name tag reads "Ben." I clock all of this before I get to him. At the same time, I check for exit doors and access points around me, points of entry were someone to sneak up on me. I'll always do this when I walk in a room. Always check my surroundings and make sure I know exactly what's coming from what direction. When I reach the desk, I see Pink lean on it and survey the room the same way I did. A product of years of training.

"Hi. I'm Drake Hart, and this is my partner, Daniel Pinkoski." I nod towards Pink. The security guard takes a step back, his eyes darting between us. "We're here with Hart Security about a disturbance in one of the homes in your building. I spoke with

Orlando here at the front desk earlier this morning about obtaining some footage."

"Orlando isn't here," he says, confirming what I already know. Orlando doesn't get in for a few more hours.

"That's fine. I'm sure you can help, Ben. I can tell you take your job seriously, and I'm also sure you wouldn't want Miss Zoey Barber to come to any harm."

He puffs out his chest a little, reversing his retreat. Bingo. I'd had a feeling this approach might work after I read the file I pulled on him. Ben here has tried to get into the police force twice. Denied twice, both times for a bad knee.

On paper he looks like a stand-up guy and might have made an okay cop.

"Orlando didn't say anything about you stopping by." He leans down, clicking on his computer a few times like he's looking for a note. I'm sure Orlando didn't tell him we'd be stopping by because he'd told us he wouldn't be handing over any tapes. Some bullshit about protecting his other tenants. That I'd need a warrant if I wanted them.

From the looks of how Orlando's running shit around here, he doesn't give a fuck about protecting his tenants. More likely he's covering his own ass because if those tapes got out, they'd show he let someone in he shouldn't have, and it'd be his ass on the line.

"I don't see anything, but I can easily get you some tapes if you'd like. Anything to help keep our Zoey safe. She's such a sweet girl. Strange but sweet."

I feel Pink's hand come down on my shoulder just before I can open my mouth.

"That'd be real helpful if you don't mind," he says, rattling off the date and times we need. He knew I was about to lay into Ben. Which would have fucked everything up. I take a deep breath and look over at Pink, who levels me with a look that I know means *get it the fuck together*.

Maybe Zoey is strange, but she's no stranger than me. Hell, what he thinks is strange about her is what I can't seem to get enough of. Everything that comes out her mouth just seems to do it for me. How someone hasn't snatched her up before now, I have no fucking idea. I have to believe what she is saying about only ever having feelings for me, because she came on so strong. If she'd done that with someone else, I can't imagine them resisting planting a ring on her finger.

"I need a ring." The words pop right out of my mouth in Zoey fashion, making Pink shake his head. The security guard continues to click away on his keyboard.

A ring on her finger sounds real nice. I can already picture her running her hands all over my body as she wears it. The thought has my cock coming to life.

"That's strange," Ben says, pulling me from the thoughts I shouldn't be having right now. I'm once again losing myself in a Zoey fog and not making sure I'm getting shit done, keeping her safe.

"What?" The word comes out a little harder then I mean it to. I'm still agitated with him, even though he's getting me what I want.

"They're gone. There's nothing on here. In fact, I can't seem to find any tapes prior to my shift today." He keeps clicking away like he might find it, but I know he won't.

"I smell shit," I tell Pink, who just nods his head.

I turn, heading out the door, not bothering to try and get more from Ben. He's got nothing. I pull out my phone and dial my office.

"Hart Security," Sherrie, Pink's youngest sister, answers the phone.

"I need a crew over at Zoey's apartment. I want prints done."

"On the door?" she questions, and I hear her typing away on her computer.

"Everywhere."

CHAPTER ELEVEN

ZOEY

"I want to tell you you're crazy, but..." Elle shrugs as she slides off the bar stool and heads for the coffee pot. "But I like how you two look together. It's different."

Different. A word I've been hearing my whole life.

"I really like him." I fiddle with the edges of the paper sitting on the counter, needing to do something with my hands. My sister's opinion means a lot to me. It's always been her and me, and while she might me bossy with me, I know I need it. She pulls me back and keeps me on track. If I didn't have her, I'd probably just live in a mess of chaos.

"I've never felt like this. I can't even seem to understand it." Not that I've really tried. My mind seems to be solely focused on Drake.

"Is that driving you crazy?" After she looks in a few cabinets, she finds a mug and makes herself a cup. She doesn't offer me one, knowing I can't stand the stuff unless it's one of those fancy ones loaded with whipped cream and chocolate. Elle just drinks hers straight black.

"No."

"Well, there you go." She smiles over her coffee cup before taking a sip.

It hasn't been driving me crazy, oddly enough. I like for things to have reason to them. With this, I just seem to be trying to snatch it up and keep it without caring about why. I was so freaking happy when he seemed to be on board with the idea of getting married. I was scared when he didn't answer me quickly at first when we were lying in bed before Elle and Pink showed up.

Or maybe he just said that so as not to embarrass me. A little bit of that sinking feeling comes back.

"He's handsome. Like those rough, buff guys women always go crazy for on TV."

"And?" She sets her coffee down, resting her elbows on the counter, and studies me like she doesn't understand what I'm getting at.

I just shrug. I've never once really thought about what I looked like, despite having a sister who was once a model. Now I care. I want us to fit.

"You two fit, Zoey," she says, like she's reading my mind, something I often think she can do. "That's why I'm not all up in your business about it. I like how he is with you. How you are with him. I've never see you like this. You seem happy."

"I thought all guys were pig-headed assholes?" I remind her of the words I'm pretty sure I heard her mutter less than a week ago.

"Most are. They just want in your pants."

"I hope so because I really want Drake in my pants," I say dreamily, and Elle spits out a mouthful of coffee, making me jump.

She wipes up her mess and shakes her head. "I meant that's all some men want, and I can't believe that just came out of your mouth. I'm liking Drake more and more by the second."

I narrow my eyes at her, making her laugh more.

"Simmer down, Zoey. I didn't mean it like that. The man clearly only has eyes for you. Trust me. I know by the way his eyes follow you that he can't seem to let you out of his reach. It's sweet. Plus, I'm not even sure he knows I have a vagina."

"Pink knows you have a vagina."

My words make her narrow her eyes on me now. I still can't believe all the things she's let him get away with. No one gives the brush off better than Elle.

"Well, he's not getting anywhere near my vagina."

"I don't know how you do it. I haven't even had sex and I think I'm already addicted to it. I'm not sure what will happen once I get it. I don't know how you go so long without it having done it before. You actually know how good it is. I was just in the dark, but now I know it's going to be awesome."

Elle silently finishes cleaning up. I can feel the tension in the air grow a little.

"You've had sex, right? I just thought..." I trail

69

off, trying to think back. She's never had a serious boyfriend, but she has dated before. Or used to date, anyways. I just never asked her about sex because, well, I never really thought much about it before now.

"Elle?" I push.

"No, I haven't had sex," she finally snaps. I can feel my eyes widen. Okay then. Didn't see that one coming.

"Like I said, men are assholes who only want in your pants, and then they move on to the next. They only like me because I'm pretty and want to say they banged me. Or they think they can buy me."

"Does Pink make you feel that way, too?" I ask, suddenly feeling bad. I'd never thought about it like that. It reminds me a little of what Drake said about me just wanting him for sex, which isn't true.

"He just makes me feel frustrated," she growls. Actually growls in a voice I've never heard her use before. It makes me giggle a little. Her eyes snap to me. It's the look she gives me when I'm saying something I shouldn't be.

"Sexually frustrated?"

"I'm going to punch you."

"What?" I throw my hands up, and she flings the towel she used to clean the mess at me. I catch it midair before tossing it back at her.

"I'm just wondering. You let him touch and kiss on you after you yell at him. It's confusing." I've never seen a man handle Elle like Pink does. It's actually really intriguing. He seems to know how to work her. Even I can't do that and I've known her my whole life.

She lets out a heavy sigh as she makes her way back to her stool.

"No, I don't feel like he just wants in my pants. Normally, when you call a guy on it they move on, but you never know. I'm jaded. He just keeps getting all in my space and kissing me like he can do it whenever he wants. It's annoying and—"

"Hot," I finish for her, making her roll her eyes, but I see the side of her mouth quirk up a little, like she's remembering him *annoying* her.

"I like him," she finally admits. "And I hate that I like him, and I hate that he seems to know I like him." She looks so frustrated at her own admission.

I giggle once again at the circle she seems to be going in.

"You should just give in and not question it, like me. My logic is undeniable," I tell her, giving her one of my favorite movie lines. I use it on her when she tries to argue a point against me. "We could do a double wedding!"

I jump up from my chair like I just came up with the best idea ever. Because I did.

"I can't even with you," she says, finally cracking a smile and laughing.

"Hey, if all he wants is in your pants, then you'll know where you stand when you say you're getting married. It's perfect." I nod my head. Damn, I might be good at the whole relationship thing after all. I could Oprah this and just start handing out marriages.

I start jumping around and chanting, "*You* get a wedding. *You* get a wedding." Elle just laughs harder.

When the door opens, I spin to see Drake and Pink are back.

"We're all getting married!" I tell them before launching myself at Drake.

CHAPTER TWELVE

DRAKE

I reach out and wrap Zoey up as she jumps into my arms. I hold her close, pressing my nose to her neck and inhaling her scent. She's sweet like fresh honeysuckle, and it drives me wild. Having her little warm body wrapped around mine makes me feel like I've come home. Fuck, I'm going to get used to coming home to this every day.

I turn towards Pink and wink at him over Zoey's shoulder. "I'll let you handle that one." I grip her ass hard as I walk towards the bedroom. "See you guys later."

I don't turn around to watch them leave. I hear the front door shut and the lock click into place just as I enter the master bedroom.

"Have you been planning our wedding?" I ask as I kiss Zoey's neck and lay her on the bed. I crawl over her, pulling at her T-shirt as she reaches for mine. I get her shirt off and look down at her, seeing her full breasts spilling out of the top of her white cotton bra.

"Yes. I think it would be cost effective if we all got married at the same time, at the same place. It would be fun," she says as she runs her hands down my naked chest.

I pull the small box out of my pocket and set it on her bare tummy. I look up into her eyes and see excitement there as she snatches the box and opens it up.

"Oh, it's so sparkly!" she exclaims, taking the ring out of the box. "I never wear jewelry, but I'll wear this all the time. It's so pretty. What is it?"

I shake my head, thinking this is the craziest proposal of all time, and I'm pretty sure she just decided Pink is getting married, too. "It's an amethyst. It's for the month that we met—February. And also my birthday month."

"It's your birthday? When?" She looks up at me excitedly, and I can't help but smile back at her.

"It's in a couple of weeks." Nervously, I take the ring from her hands and slide it onto her finger. "I wanted as much of me on you as possible, and I thought was perfect. I found it in an antique store on the way back here today. I needed you to have my ring on you to show the world that you're mine."

She looks down at it and then back at me, smiling bigger than I've ever seen. "It's beautiful. Thank you so much, Drake."

Hearing her say the words releases any remaining nerves I had. If she didn't like it or she didn't want to do this, she would have told me. I know that she'll only tell me the truth about how she feels.

Leaning down, I keep my lips just a breath from hers and whisper the words I've been dying to say since the moment I laid eyes on her.

"I love you, Zoey."

"I love you, too, Drake."

Feeling the words hit my lips at the same time they hit my heart is all consuming. I can't stand even the millimeter of distance between us, so I connect our lips. Our kiss is fierce, and our passion escalates as the truth between us settles into place.

It's beyond rhyme or reason how this happened so fast. It's hard to believe it was even possible. But it is. This is unlike anything I've ever felt, and I want to cling to it and never let it go. Life is so goddamn short, and the world could end tomorrow. Everything in my arms could disappear, and I don't want regret left on the table. I want to know that nothing remains unsaid to Zoey and that nothing is held back.

As our tongues meet and taste one another and as Zoey runs her hand down my back, I feel the cool band of the ring on her finger against my skin. It's a reminder that she's mine. Forever.

She breaks our kiss and reaches down between us, undoing my jeans and pushing them down my hips.

"I want sex now, Drake." She licks her lips and smiles at me as her small hand reaches into my jeans and wraps around my cock.

"Fuck." I bury my face against her cleavage, trying not to cum on her hand from just the slight touch.

"We're getting married. You can't back out," she says, stroking my cock up and down.

"Easy, baby." I reach down, gently grabbing her wrist and taking it off my cock. I bring her hand to my mouth and kiss the palm. "It's going to be over far too soon if you keep that up."

Before she can protest any further, I reach behind her and unhook her bra, letting her big breasts spill out. My mouth goes directly to her nipple as her fingers go to my hair, and a moan escapes her lips.

"Wow, that feels good."

I reach down between us and undo her jeans, pushing them and her panties down. I let her nipple out of my mouth with a pop as I move down her body, getting her naked and kicking off the rest of my clothes at the same time.

When I go to move back up her body, I push her legs apart and kiss my way up her thigh. "Just one kiss before, Zoey," I whisper against her tender skin as I put my mouth on her pussy and give it a few licks.

I slip my fingers up the inside of her thigh and to her wet opening. I slide one in and feel her clench down on me. She's unbelievably tight, and I know she's going to squeeze the life out of me when I get my cock in there.

Zoey moans again as I give her long firm licks, tasting her pussy and feeling where I'm about to fit inside her. Slipping another finger inside her, I work them in and out, trying to stretch her as much as possible. I feel her hymen give a little as I rock in and out of her with my fingers. When I bring a third to her opening, I pull my mouth back from her clit.

"This might sting a bit, cupcake. But I want to get you ready for me." I look up and see her nod as she runs her fingers through my hair.

Her cheeks are flushed, her mouth partly open as quick breaths puff in and out. She's ready for some kind of release, and I hope to give it to her at the same time the pain comes so I can take away the hurt.

I lower my mouth back to her clit and suck it into my mouth, flicking my tongue across it. Her sweet honeysuckle scent fills my lungs, and I moan around her pussy as I plunge three thick fingers into her.

I hear her cry out from her orgasm and the bite of pain as I gently move them in and out of her body. Her tight pussy clamps down on me, and I feel her hymen break as her climax hits her.

Having a mouth full of her pussy as the cool sheets rub against my dick is almost too much. It takes everything inside me to hold back from cumming all over myself while I help her ride out her pleasure and give her body time to adjust to the invasion.

I rub her G spot, making her climax last longer as I give her clit soft licks. After a few minutes of loving her pussy, she relaxes under me, and her legs fall open carelessly.

I look up to see a huge smile on her face, and I can't help but smile back.

She lifts her hips a little as I move my fingers again. I look down and see just a small trace of her virginity on them, and I'm overwhelmed by the desire to taste it. I pull my fingers from her body and put them into my mouth, licking them clean. I can taste the tinge of copper, as well as the sweetness of her pussy, flavored by the orgasm she gave me. I feel like the act binds us together. She'll forever be mine.

After I take the fingers from my mouth, I lean down and give her pussy a few more licks before I move up her body. I don't want to leave her sweet taste, but my cock is a greedy bastard and he wants a taste, too.

"Drake," Zoey moans, pulling me to her.

My mouth immediately goes for her hard nipple, needing it in my mouth as my cock lines up at her opening.

"Please, Drake. I need more."

As if to punctuate her statement, she raises her hips, letting the tip of my cock dip into her wetness. Giving her what she wants, I push forward past her damp folds and let her pussy suck me into her tight channel.

She's so goddamn tight, and I bite down a little on her nipple to keep myself from cumming. The distraction of pleasing her body is enough to keep me from the edge, and I thrust all the way inside her as she clenches around me.

Breaking my mouth away from her breast, I look up into her eyes and start to thrust in and out of her in long strokes.

"I won't last long," I grit out, trying not to cum too soon.

"I'm so excited," she says, looking up at me with big bright eyes. "Will I feel the cum go in me?"

Her words have me nearly losing it, and I bury my face in her neck. "Fuck, Zoey. You're going to make me cum."

"I'm just wondering if I'll feel it when it happens. Will I get really full? Like, is there room in me for that? Your cock is ginormous. I don't know how cum will fit, too. I should cum on your cock first to see what that feels like. Cumming on your fingers was spectacular."

I smile against her neck and pump in and out of her. When I reach between us and rub her clit, she moans in my ear.

"Oh, that's it. Yep, I'm there."

I softly bite down on her shoulder as she clenches around me. I feel her nails scratch down my back as she tenses up and lets out her orgasm. My name leaves her lips, and it's then I can't hold back any more.

The sound of her cumming, combined with her uttering my name, is all I can take, and I thrust into her one final time, filling her with every drop of me.

I grunt against her body as wave after wave of pleasure shoots up my spine, through my balls. It's the most intense orgasm of my life, and I nearly collapse on Zoey as I reach the end of it.

Bracing myself on my elbows, I keep myself buried inside her as I catch my breath.

"Wow. I totally felt that," she says, kissing my neck. "Oh."

The funny sound has me leaning up to look down at her.

"I feel it running down my ass. Is that normal? You must have cum a lot. Do I have to clean up? I kind of like you being inside me like this. Is that weird?"

I smile as I roll us over, keeping my cock in her. Fuck, I love the things that just come out of her mouth. No embarrassment. Just her. Once she's settled on top of me, I hold her hips and thrust up inside her.

"I don't know what's normal and if everyone likes what we like. But I know that there's nothing about you that I don't want to taste or love. And hearing you say that you like me inside you makes me want to fuck you all over again."

She beams at me like I just made her world right, and she starts to move up and down on my cock.

"Good, because I want to do that again, and this time with more positions. I'm pretty flexible." She leans forward a little. "I Googled some stuff," she says seriously.

My smile turns into a moan as she leans back a little and takes me deeper inside her. If the world ends now, I'll die a happy man.

CHAPTER THIRTEEN

ZOEY

"Don't even think about it, cupcake," Drake says as I eye him over the breakfast bar while he cleans up after our late lunch.

Another knock sounds at the door, and I make my move, darting for it as quick as I can. I only make it four steps before he has me in his arms, throwing me over his shoulder as I squeal. Over the past few weeks I've noticed I like to make him chase me. There's something about the thrill of it. I can't seem to stop myself, and I knew the moment I heard the knock at the front door that it was another chance to strike.

I'm not allowed to answer the door. Hell, I haven't even left this place in over two weeks. Held up in a Drake sex fog. It wasn't until recently that I noticed how lost I'd become in him. I wasn't wrapping up a current project I was working on and Elle kept reminding me of it daily. Probably because Ensore, the company we had a contract with right now, was all over her about it and making her hound me.

Drake swats my ass, making me wiggle and laugh.

"I don't know why you even try. I'll always catch you."

He turns a little so he doesn't not knock me against the door as he checks the peephole. It has to be someone from inside the building or a call would have rung up. The only visitors we get are Pink and Elle. If I had to guess, it's Elle, and that means Pink isn't far behind. He just kind of pops up when she's around, making sure to always be in her space. She'll snap at him and then they go at it, and it always ends with Pink carrying her out of the apartment, my sister wrapped around him. I have no clue how Pink can walk and make out at the same time, but he seems to have it down to an art.

"Elle," Drake says, sliding me down his big body until my bare feet hit the floor. Even knowing it's my sister, he still blocks the door with his body as he lets her in, not even letting me see the hallway, an easy feat with his Hulk-sized body.

Elle pushes in, not waiting to be invited.

"You got it all done?" she huffs, and I just stare at her. She doesn't look her normal self. In fact, she looks like I look after a long night with Drake. Her blonde hair is messy, her normally perfectly-pressed dress shirt looks like it was picked up off the floor and just thrown on.

"You said I'd have it by now," she goes on. I know she's frustrated with me. I keep telling her I'm almost done but then get distracted. She doesn't want us to look flaky.

"It's Drake's fault. I told him I had to work and he wouldn't let me leave the bed." I stretch the truth and push him towards her, but he doesn't move. Freaking concrete boulder.

"Yeah, because I'm going to peel your sweet ass off me when you wrap yourself around me."

I totally did do that this morning. Normally, Drake wakes up before me to go work out, but this morning I somehow woke before him. Needless to say, he didn't go to the gym this morning. I also didn't finish my coding for Ensore's new system.

"God, if I didn't love the look you put on my sister's face, I'd want to smack you both for being so annoyingly adorable."

"You're one to talk," I shoot back at her.

"Hey, I'm just using him for sex."

"I knew it! You did it!" I point my finger at her. She hasn't given me anything about what's going on between her and Pink except for the make-out sessions I've seen, but I haven't seen a ton of her these past two weeks. I turn my pointer finger to Drake. "Double wedding is back on."

Drake grabs my finger before biting the end of it, then kissing it. "You want your double wedding, I'll make sure you get it, cupcake."

"Drake says I can have anything I want," I confirm to Elle.

"Is that so?" She crosses her arms and looks at me with a doubtful expression.

I just nod because it's true. There's not one thing I've asked for that I haven't gotten. But all I seem to ask for is orgasms and food. Oh, and all *The X-Files* on Blu-ray.

"Can you make Pink stop following me around?" She raises an eyebrow, knowing that maybe Drake could make Pink leave her alone. He's Pink's boss, but I don't think Drake telling him to leave her alone would work.

"Veto!" I yell before leaning towards Drake. "I can veto stuff, right?"

"Yeah, cupcake, you can veto stuff."

"See?" I nod again, confirming that I get whatever I want. I think I'm more poking Elle than anything because before Drake she would have been all, "Why do you need *The X-Files* on Blu-ray? They are all on Netflix."

"Code, Zoey. I'm not joking anymore. We signed a contract."

"Okay, okay. I can have it all wrapped up in a few hours. It's all done. I just want to run a few more tests on it."

"Thank you."

"When I'm done, do you want to start planning our double wedding? I found these board things that you pin stuff to online called Pinterest. WeddingMama1245 told me all the good places to find stuff to pin."

"WeddingMama1245?" Elle says, laughing.

"She's no joke. Don't let the name fool you," I

say. I only tried to question WeddingMama1245 on something the other day and she snapped at me, saying she wasn't going to give me links anymore. I thought about just hacking her and seeing what she was looking at, but I just said sorry instead. I didn't want to lose my WeddingMama1245 connection.

"I wasn't done with you." I hear a growl and turn to see Pink standing in the doorway wearing only a pair of shorts. He looks like he just got out of the shower.

"You're such a caveman. You don't dismiss me," Elle retorts.

"I'll show you caveman when I get that baby planted in you."

"I can't believe you just said that." Elle's words come out all breathy. The same way mine do when Drake gives me his predatory eyes that I know are going to have me flat on my back in about two seconds.

"You're right. It might already be in there." Pink smiles at the statement, seeming to like the idea. A lot. Then he's grabbing for her. She doesn't even try to dodge him. She just lets him pick her up and rolls her eyes as he carries her out.

Drake shuts the door behind them, locking it.

"Pink always like that?" I ask, wondering about what he just said. Implying he was trying to impregnate my sister.

"Fuck no." Drake points to the door. "That, I've never seen before. He's done."

"How do you know?" I push, wanting confirmation that Pink is good for my sister.

"I know the look, cupcake. See it every time I look in the mirror. He's in love with her, and he's making sure she can never leave him."

I wrap my arms around him and hug him tightly.

"You start that and your sister will be back here in a few hours asking if you got your stuff done."

I lean back and look up at him.

"Fine, fine, fine. I'll do it. But when I'm done, you're mine for the night."

"I'm always yours, cupcake." He kisses me on the nose. "Go get your stuff and meet me in the office. We'll both knock out some work. I've got some things I need to go over."

I just nod and pull away. I don't ask what it is he has to go over. If he doesn't tell me, then it's mostly my case. I wish we could just find the stupid stalker already. I know it's driving him crazy and making him edgy. To top it off, I'm starting to get cabin fever. I didn't even know that was possible because I love staying in, but two weeks of not going outside is starting to wear on me. I don't even ask Drake if he'll take me out because he would, but I know it would stress him out and ruin the trip.

I go to our bedroom and grab my laptop and a few folders before making my way back to his office. Drake is sitting in his big chair and going through paperwork. He glances up. "Sit anywhere you want, cupcake," he says, then goes back to his papers.

I make my way over to him, crawling into his lap and opening up my laptop. I push a few of his papers to the side before I set it down on the desk in front of me.

"Comfy?" he laughs.

"You said anywhere, and this looked like the best spot to me."

He wraps one arm around my waist, pulling me back a little and adjusting my position slightly.

"That I did." He picks up another paper with his free hand, and we both get back to work.

CHAPTER FOURTEEN

DRAKE

As the sun sets and Zoey finishes her coding, she shuts her laptop with a satisfied sigh. I finished my work a little bit ago, but I just kept my arms wrapped around her while she worked. She got so consumed with her project I didn't want to disturb her, and I know she needed to work.

"All finished?" I ask, leaning in and kissing her neck. Her sweet honeysuckle smell fills my lungs, and I close my eyes as I press my nose against her soft skin.

"All finished," she confirms.

Before she can say anything else, I scoop her up and carry her out of the office.

"Orgasms?" she asks brightly on the way to the bedroom, and I smile back at her, knowing she was going to ask that.

"Orgasms," I answer, always giving her what she wants.

Laying her down on the bed, I strip off her loose top and leggings. She's completely naked underneath, and it takes me only a second to kick off my T-shirt and shorts. Being able to laze around the house all day with Zoey, even while working, has been wonderful. Being able to sneak my hand up her shirt any time I want to get a handful of her breasts is heaven.

Once I've got us undressed, I lean down and kiss her belly and across her hips. Her legs fall open, and she puts her hands behind her head, just waiting on me to pleasure her. Smiling against her skin, I do what she wants, kissing her soft belly and curvy hips.

Reaching down to her thighs, I grab the thick flesh there and dig my fingers in. The little dimples on the backs of her legs are adorable, and I move down to bite her there.

She giggles as I run my tongue along her legs, not leaving an inch untouched.

"I love you, Zoey," I whisper to her calf as I throw it over my shoulder and kiss her there.

Not waiting for her response, I press my cock to her opening and thrust all the way inside her. I grind against her, rubbing her clit, and she lets out a long moan of pleasure.

She's on her back with one leg down on the bed and one over my shoulder. I hold myself inside her, just grinding down on her clit while my cock throbs inside of her.

"I love you, too, Drake," she breathes out, clutching the sheets beside her.

Long gone is the look of relaxed pleasure on her face. Now she's tense with need and getting closer to the edge.

I lean forward a little, putting more pressure on her clit and opening her up further, her leg still draped over my shoulder.

As I rub the base of my cock right against her clit, she mewls with want, inching towards her peak. My dick is being squeezed by her sweet pussy pulses, and it's all I can do to hold on to my cum. I need her to go first, and then I'll follow her.

I move my hips against her, not pulling out or inching away. Just back and forth, rubbing her hard nub in perfect pulses.

"That's it. Cum for me, cupcake. Cum all over my cock while lying still, just like this." Her pussy clenches, and I feel her peak is close. "That's it, almost there." I pulse my cock inside her, letting her feel just how hard I am while rubbing back and forth just a few more times.

"So beautiful," I whisper as she hits her climax and her back bows off the bed. Her orgasm takes over, and she cums hard on my cock. Her pussy clamps down on me, and I follow her over, spilling my seed deep inside her as we both find our pinnacles of pleasure.

I gently bring her leg down from my shoulder and lie on top of her body. It's then I start to lazily thrust in and out of her, feeling the wetness of our combined passion spread between us.

We both came from my just being inside her. Our slow, easy love-making sets a perfect pace, and it's welcomed after our hard orgasms. Neither of us is in a hurry to end the night now. It's only the beginning.

I look down at the scars covering various parts of my skin, my tatted-up arms wrapped around her as her flawless body lays draped over me. We're so different when I lay my skin against hers, but we couldn't possibly fit together any better. If you'd have told me a month ago I'd be this wrapped up in a woman, that I didn't think I'd be able to breathe without one, I would've laughed.

The soft sweet girls like Zoey never hit on me. It was always the ones who looked a little rough around the edges. Maybe they thought I'd dish out a little pain with what they wanted. To have someone like Zoey wrapped around me feels like coming home every morning. Waking to find her pressed against me like a second skin is bliss.

I fucking love it. I don't think I could ever live without it now that I've had a taste of her. To have a little family of my own and belong to someone. That's why I have to get this stalker shit dealt with. More emails have come, but Zoey doesn't know about them. Her sister is getting even more freaked out, and I don't blame her because of the rate at which the stalker is accelerating. She's calling me about three times a day. Luckily, we're on the same page, and we don't want to stress Zoey out, so we leave her in the dark. I actually think she thinks the threat is gone because I don't bring it up. I don't want to bring it up because I don't want that shit touching her. I thank fuck that Pink has seemed to be able to keep Elle calmed down about it all. The emails have started getting to an extreme sexual level that makes me want to paint the walls in the blood of whoever this fuck is. He seems to be freaking out that he can't have eyes on Zoey now that she is locked away safe in our home. He's even started mentioning me in his little fucked-up love notes. He is getting sloppy, which is good news for me. Sloppy gets caught. I just don't want that slop touching my girl.

She's so soft and sweet and coated with an innocence I don't want her to lose. I will be the hard to her soft. If something needs to hit us, it'll hit me alone. I want to be her shield.

I know this shit has something to do with her work, and the stalker's obsession with her has started to morph into some fucked-up crush or adoration for her. I can't blame the guy for wanting her, but she's mine and nothing will take her from me. I want this shit squashed. I knew I could only keep her locked up in this condo so long, and the days are ticking by. Luckily, her sister is close and that's helping keep her sweet ass planted at home.

Slowly, I unwrap myself from her body, sliding out from under her and pulling myself from the bed. Leaning down, I kiss her bare back before brushing the hair out of her face. I can't help but stare at her. I keep thinking this driving need to touch her and be close to her will fade, but it doesn't. In fact, I think it's getting worse.

I shake my head at all these sappy feelings I seem to have all the time nowadays. I make my way to the bathroom, stopping to pick up littered clothes and random things Zoey seems to throw around. That's something else I oddly like. I get off on seeing her shit all over the place, and I get off even more on putting it back where it belongs because it means she lives here. Her stuff belongs with mine.

Making quick work in the bathroom, I slip on some workout clothes before heading to the kitchen. I grab a banana and text one of my men to come stand at the door while I go for a run. I write Zoey a quick note about going to the office we have in the building, even though I'll likely be back before she wakes up. As I slip out the door, I come face to face with Pink.

"Got a lead you're going to want to see." He holds up a file, and I snatch it from him.

I open it up and read the name of a company I've never even heard of before: Green Shore. "Who is this? This name hasn't come up in anything."

One of the first things we did when we took on the job was look into anyone who might be after the company she is currently consulting for. This company isn't in competition with Ensore.

"Brand new. They're going after some government contract that Ensore has tied up. It's not really a competition for them. Unless they fuck something up."

I flip through the folder before heading for the elevator. Pink follows me. I hit the button for the bottom floor and keep reading over everything.

"She's the easiest target. That's how I look at it.

She's the easiest to get to. She's just creating the encryption software for a new round of satellites that are being launched midsummer. If the encryption is messed up, no way will Ensore get the project. They'd be done for," Pink says.

I shut the folder when the elevator hits the ground floor, trying to process everything.

"And I'm sure Green Shore already has their own system set up. They'll pitch that when Ensore fails," I say, looking over to Pink.

"From what I gathered, yes. All they need is an invitation to pitch it."

"So what are we thinking here? Green Shore hired someone to break into Zoey's and get their hands on whatever it is she's doing? Either fuck it up or find a way to fuck it up later?"

"In the simplest terms, yeah. I don't understand half the shit."

"Me neither," I say, making my way down the hallway before opening the door to our offices. I'm thankful that I'd chosen to turn one of the condos in the building into our offices. Now I'd always be close to home, where Zoey would be since she worked from home mainly. Or maybe I could put her a desk in my office down here for her. I really liked that idea. I'd watched Zoey work last night, and I couldn't make head or tail of anything she was doing. All I saw were lines and lines of numbers, but she could easily do that down here in my office. Our office.

Sherrie pops up from behind her desk as we enter the offices.

"I need a list of all employees at a company called

Green Shore." I hand her the folder. "I also want a list of their family members and close friends. Look hard into anyone with a criminal past, no matter how small. I even want to know if they have sealed records from when they were snot-nosed kids, and I want those records unsealed. Call in favors, I don't give a shit."

"How fast you want it?" she asks, dropping the folder on her desk and sitting down.

"Call a few of your sisters to help, and use any of the men if you need leg work." I hear Pink sigh behind me. He hates when his sisters come in to help out. They might run their mouths a lot when they're in here, but they get shit done. No one multi-tasks like a woman.

"So…yesterday."

"Yeah," I confirm because whoever they hired to get what they wanted from Zoey has lost control of that person. Things are bound to be sloppy, and it's going to make it a whole lot easier to figure out who it is.

CHAPTER FIFTEEN

ZOEY

I open one eye to see Elle lying in bed with me.

"You're naked," she says, and I bury my head back in my pillow, feeling the bed shake as she laughs.

"What are you doing?" I ask, pulling the covers fully over myself while rolling to my side to look at her. She's completely made up in a gray pencil skirt and pink silk blouse. She has on make-up and her hair is styled. I'm surprised she isn't worried about wrinkling her outfit. She must have a meeting or something today.

"How's this place so clean with you living in it?" Elle rolls to her side, too, looking at me and ignoring my question.

"Is it?" I lean up and look around the room. I hadn't really noticed, but it's oddly clean for a space that I've been living in.

"He cleans, too? You hit the man jackpot." She reaches out and tucks my hair behind my ear.

"He really is perfect, isn't he?" I can't help but agree with her. Because Drake *is* perfect. Perfect for me. It's like we're made for each other, and he likes all my odd little quirks. In fact, they seem to turn him on.

"They are something," she agrees, dropping back down on the bed and looking up at the ceiling. She's finally admitting her feelings for Pink.

"So you admit it." I smile at her, making her roll her eyes, but I see right through her. "Why are you denying it so much?" I don't get it. I wanted Drake and I just went for it. Seems like the logical thing to me.

"Because I didn't want it at first. The attraction was fast, and I'd never felt anything like it before. I've been burned a few times with guys who didn't have good intentions."

I knew she had been. It's why she stopped even trying with guys anymore. Elle always wanted a big family with a white picket fence and a house full of babies. A big family. It's something I'm sure Pink could give her if she let him. He's got family popping out from everywhere.

"But I like him teasing me. I know I can be a little much with how I like things done and everything in order. Initially, I thought my personally would drive him away, but he just kind of steamrolls over me, and I like it when he does. Is that stupid?" She throws one arm over her eyes "*Grr*. I don't know."

I just laugh. I've never seen Elle so out of sorts before. I like it, too.

"I don't really think it matters what you do at this point. I'm pretty sure he's said over and over that you're his and you're not going anywhere. Soooo..." I shrug.

She just smiles.

"Never thought I'd see the day we fell for a couple of friends."

"Double wedding," I say again. I want to ask her about the comment Pink made about knocking her up, but I don't want to push it.

She rolls out of the bed and brushes her hands over her clothes.

"You have to personally deliver the package to Ensore. They want it straight from your hands to theirs."

I let out a sigh. I figured that was probably the case, especially when no one came for it yesterday.

"I'm giving them the whole laptop, but I haven't left this place in over two weeks. I'll need to talk to Drake."

I roll over and grab my phone from the side table.

"There's a note in the kitchen that says he was going for a run."

I look at the clock and know he should be back by now.

I slide my finger across the screen and read the text

Hulk: Have to work, cupcake. I'll see you

tonight.

"He's working," I inform Elle, who's now slipping on her heels.

"Yeah, Pink slipped out quick this morning, too. They must have something going on."

"Well, crap. How are we going to take the laptop in?"

"I'm sure one of the guys on the door will escort us or something. Ensore isn't that far away. Maybe only a mile."

"Alright. Let me get dressed and I'll meet you in the kitchen." Elle leaves the room, and I make quick work of getting ready in the bathroom. I slide on a pair of jeans, hoodie, and sneakers. Elle let go of my having to dress *professional* a long time ago.

When I enter the kitchen, Elle is typing away on her phone. She doesn't even look up when she speaks. "I told them we'd be by shortly and to have someone there to take the laptop."

"Sounds good." I open the pantry door and don't see anything I want to eat, or at least anything I feel like making. Drake has spoiled me with his cooking.

"You think we can go to Bojo's after? I'm starving."

"God, that sounds so good. We haven't eaten there in forever." By *forever* she means maybe two weeks, which is a long time for us. We normally eat there about three to four times a week. It's a simple diner, but they have anything and everything you could want.

"Cool." I grab my bag and slip my laptop and

phone inside. Elle follows me to the door. When I open the door, I'm surprised that no one is standing outside. Normally, if Drake isn't here, he has a guy who just stands there looking extremely intimidating.

"That's odd." I look up and down the hallway, and Elle does the same.

"There was someone here when I came in. Maybe there isn't a threat anymore and that's what the guys have been up to this morning."

"Maybe," I mumble, digging into my bag for my phone.

"Front left pocket."

I reach into the front left pocket of my bag and pull out my phone. I tap out a message to Drake.

Me: No guard on the door. I need to drop laptop off at Ensore.

I hit send and wait for a response, but nothing comes.

"Crap. I don't want to bother him if he's busy. I've been hogging all of his time."

Elle fiddles with her own phone for a moment before sighing.

"Let's just pop into Drake and Pink's office downstairs real quick and see if there is someone who can take us over there. It's not that far. I'm sure one of them can pull themselves away for a little while to run us over.."

"Alright," I agree, shooting Drake another text to at least let him know I'm on my way down to his office.

We ride silently down the elevator and when it gets to the bottom floor, I only take two steps out before I'm slammed back against a wall.

My head hits the wall hard, and my bag slips from my hands. I hear Elle scream, and black dots swim before me as I try to get my bearings.

"Orlando?" It's then I realize the man who has me against the wall is one of the security guards at my old building. He's so close I can feel his warm breath on my skin. His eyes seem wild as they dart back and forth.

"You had to fuck everything up. I could've just planted the bug in your computer and made me a shitload of money. But no, you have to get these other fuckers involved," he growls at me.

I see Elle trying to pull at him, but it doesn't seem to be doing any good. He turns around, giving her a shove and sending her sprawling to the floor.

"Who would have thought it would be so hard to get your attention? One would think it would be easy. Give the chubby, geeky girl a little attention and I should've been in your place like," he snaps his fingers, "that. But no. It was like I didn't even exist." He leans in a little more, and I stop breathing. I can smell the stench of alcohol on his breath. "But you spread your legs for the other guy, didn't you? You like them big and all scarred up? Is that what gets you off?" He licks up the side of my face, and I feel my stomach roil.

I push at his chest and he goes flying, hitting the floor a whole lot harder than Elle did.

I look up as Drake peels him from the floor like

he's nothing more than a rag doll, before punching him right in the face. The crunch of cracking bone is sickeningly loud.

This Hulk joke is really starting to become a reality.

"Drake, man, stop. You kill him and your ass will be in jail," Pink says, coming to stand in front of Drake. He stops him from going to pick Orlando up again, holding his hands out to block him.

Drake's whole body is tight, his breathing heavy. Pink's eyes dart to mine, and I can read what he wants.

I walk up behind Drake and wrap my arms around him, resting my head against his back. I can feel some of the tension leave his body at the contact.

Then I hear the sirens.

CHAPTER SIXTEEN

DRAKE

I rest my hands on top of Zoey's. I don't take my eyes off Orlando for a second while the cops come in and get things sorted out.

They wanted to question us separately, but Zoey wouldn't let me go, and I wasn't about to take my hands off her while things were still getting settled.

Pink and I were at my office when his sisters came in and got to work. I don't know how but one of them was able to find the deleted security footage from Zoey's apartment. At the same time, we found a name we'd come across before. Orlando Davies popped up as working with Green Shore before coming to work in Zoey's building, and that's when it all clicked into place.

My phone buzzed just as this all happened, and I checked it to see Zoey's messages. There was no reason security shouldn't have been at her door, so I called some of my old partners at the station and had them come to the building for back up.

When I got downstairs and I saw Orlando's hands on Zoey, red flooded my vision, and I just went into attack mode. It's all still a little fuzzy from the rage and adrenaline. It was like nothing I'd ever felt before, and I've been in a lot of crazy situations when I worked SWAT. But all I remember was needing to get him off of her. I also remember Pink running over to help Elle, and that made me angrier. The thought that someone would hurt her sister, someone Zoey loves, infuriated me.

Thankfully, Pink was able to get between us, and Zoey's touch calmed me down. I would have very likely killed him for coming near my woman. The cops arrived and arrested Orlando. Now they're just taking statements.

"We still need to deliver the files," Elle says, walking over to where we are. She looked at little shaken at first, but now she's leaning on Pink, and I can see that she's getting it back together. She's a tough one, but seeing her holding on to him is definitely a sign in the right direction.

The elevator opens behind us, and a group of cops help out Matt, the security guy we had planted outside my home.

We talk with him and the cops for a bit and find out that Orlando admitted to having slipped something into the guard's coffee. It took just long enough for Elle to get inside before he was out cold, and Orlando stashed his body in a hall closet.

With that confession, he's going to be in jail for quite some time. Matt is a decorated veteran, and I know my boys will make sure he's taken care of. Orlando may have started out as a petty criminal, but money makes people do crazy shit. It was enough to convince Orlando that coming after my woman was a good idea. God knows what he would have done to my Zoey.

The shiver snaking down my spine is stopped when Zoey's warm hand rubs my back. I squeeze her closer to me, needing the reassurance that she's still alive and still with me.

"I love you. You're right. I love you."

Zoey and I turn around to see Elle standing in front of Pink, admitting what we all knew.

"So you gonna wear my ring now?" he asks, looking into her eyes.

She puts her hands on her hips and glares at him. After a second, she lets out a huff and pushes a strand of hair out of her face. "Yes."

Pink gets down on one knee and pulls out a box. It's the one he bought the same day I got Zoey's. I squeeze her hand a little, feeling the cool band on her finger, and it makes me smile.

Elle puts her hands over her mouth, looking down at the simple gold band with little pink diamonds all around it. Pink could have gotten her a 50-carat diamond, but he knew Elle, and he knew this would mean more to her.

"One diamond for every baby I'm gonna give you, *Prinzessin*," Pink says, waiting for Elle to answer.

I wrap my arms around Zoey as we watch the

tears stream down Elle's face and she launches herself at Pink. They're kind of adorable, those two.

"Double wedding!" Zoey shouts and fist pumps the air.

"Whatever you want, cupcake," I say, kissing her forehead. "Let's get this shit delivered so I can take you upstairs and we can talk about your punishment."

"Punishment?" She looks up at me with big eyes, then smiles.

I have a feeling she won't take this lesson seriously.

CHAPTER SEVENTEEN

ZOEY

Before the door even shuts fully, Drake's big hands are cupping my face, his mouth coming down on mine. His tongue pushes into my mouth, commanding me to open for him. I can taste the sweet desperation he pours into it. I can feel his pain and worry. All the emotions he's been holding back while we finished everything come through the kiss. That this man loves me makes my heart squeeze.

He pulls away, resting his forehead against mine.

"I can't lose you, cupcake. Fuck, I swear I've never been so scared in my life than when I saw his hands on you."

He closes his eyes like he's in pain and seeing it all over again. I rub my hands against his chest, trying to calm him.

"Like the Hulk would ever let something happen

to me," I tease, making a half-smile pull at his lips.

"I love you so damn much. You're my family now. I need you. I need this. I haven't been so fucking happy in my life, and to think it could have been taken from me today... It makes me want to—"

"I'm here, Drake. No one is taking me from you," I reassure him, rubbing my hands up and down his chest, trying to calm him.

"Tell me you'll never leave me."

"Never," I say instantly. I can feel his body relax at my words. Then he starts peppering kisses all over my face. It makes me giggle. I can't even imagine what we look like together. This big, scarred, and tattooed man leaning down over me, cupping my face, placing kisses everywhere he can. It makes me melt.

My phone starts to ring, and Drake grunts in annoyance.

I swing my bag around from my shoulder and start digging through it. It's probably my sister. I just left her minutes ago. What she could need already, I have no idea. I'm shocked Pink has let her up for air to even use the phone.

"Front left pocket," Drake mutters, and I can tell he's not happy about being interrupted. I reach into the pocket and pull it out. The name *Brett – Ensore* shows across the screen. Elle must have programed the number into my phone in the event I had any questions I needed to ask when I was working on the project, and I actually hear Drake growl. A god's honest growl coming from deep in his chest.

"That was sexy," I say, looking up at him, but his

eyes are still narrowed on my phone.

He grabs it from my hand and answers it.

"Zoey's husband. How can I help you?"

I look at him in confusion. We aren't married yet. I see his jaw visibly clench.

"Yes, she's married. Did you not see the ring on her finger?" He does the growl thing again. I look down at the ring and smile. I did have it on when we dropped off the laptop. It is kind of big and hard to miss.

"No, she won't be working with your company again. Call her phone again and I'll come down there." He pulls the phone away from his ear and hits the *end* button. Elle would be so mad if she heard that. I usually don't talk to clients much. That's her job. I'm actually surprised the guy has my number. All calls usually go straight to Elle.

"Fuck. For a smart guy, he can't take a fucking clue." He slips my phone into his own pocket like he doesn't want to give it back to me.

I look at him in bewilderment.

"First time I take you out of the house and someone is hitting on you. A fucking billionaire at that." He shakes his head before running his hands through his short hair, looking a little stressed again.

"What are you talking about?"

"The man was hitting on you when we dropped off the laptop, and he just called to try to get you to go out with him."

"No, he called to offer me another job, which isn't surprising. I'm quite good at what I do."

He shakes his head like he can't believe what I'm

saying. "Elle is right." he states, confusing me further.

"Yes, she usually is," I agree, because, well, she is.

"You don't even see it."

I look around the room to try to understand what he's talking about. "See what?"

A half-laugh leaves him, pulling my eyes back to him. "Elle said men hit on you all the time and you just don't see it. Never give them the time of day."

"What? That's not true. No one hits on me."

He grabs me by the hips, lifting me up. I drop my bag, and all its contents loudly clatter to the floor. My legs go around his waist, my arms around his neck.

"It's alright that you don't see it, cupcake. You keep not seeing it, because you're about to marry a bodyguard, and I'll make sure those fuckers don't get anywhere near what's mine."

I smile, wiggling against him.

"You were jealous?" I question, liking the idea of him getting jealous over me. Now that I think about it, I'm not sure I'd like some woman calling his phone, either.

"Cupcake, I'm jealous of everything when it comes to you. The food you eat, that computer that you can stare at for hours, anything that takes your attention from me." His mouth comes to mine, and he kisses me deeply. "Jealous of these fucking clothes that get to be wrapped around your sweet, lush body all day," he says against my lips.

"Then you should probably rip them off me," I say, taking his mouth in an even deeper kiss.

I feel my back hit the bed, and he starts to rip my

clothes from me, Hulk-style.

"I don't want women calling your phone, either." I feel him laugh against my neck as he places open-mouthed kisses there.

I give him a smack on his giant bicep.

"Cupcake, I don't talk to many women except Pink's sisters," he informs me before taking my earlobe into his mouth and sucking it, making me moan his name.

"Would never even think about another woman now that I've tasted you. Fuck, who am I kidding? I knew no one else would ever do when your picture landed on my desk. Lit up my world. I was going through the motions and didn't even realize how lonely I was until you came into my life. Made me want something I didn't know I needed. Even if you left me, I'd spend every moment of my life trying to get you back. But I won't let that happen. I'd never let you come close to thinking about leaving me." I hear a click, then feel metal around my wrist, then hear another click. "No one could ever give me what you have. I wouldn't even try to replace you. I'd just spend my days and nights trying to get you back."

He leans up, looking down at me, his eyes all soft. I can feel tears pool in my eyes. No one has ever made me feel so normal and so extraordinary at the same time.

"You'll never be rid of me."

I go to wrap my arms around his, and it's then I notice I'm cuffed to the bed. My eyes widen.

"I'm going to show you just how much you do for me. Only you. You'll never question what you mean to me." His mouth comes down on mine, and like every day of the rest of our lives, he shows me just how much I mean to him.

EPILOGUE

DRAKE

5 years later...

"That's disgusting. I won't eat it."

"Yeah, me neither. It smells gross," Zoey adds, pushing her plate an inch away from her.

I lay my head in my hands and pray for strength. My wife and my almost-five-year-old daughter will surely be the death of me. Never mind the fact that Zoey is nine months pregnant with our second girl, and it's only going to get worse.

"Girls. It's just a vegetable medley. Why don't you both try it?"

Zoey looks over at Amelia and shrugs her shoulders. Amelia lets out a deep breath, and they nod to one another, as if agreeing to take one for the team.

I bite my lip to keep from smiling as they both try what I made for dinner. I try to cook healthy for all of us, but sometimes my efforts are wasted. I've somewhat retired from the security firm, only coming in to make sure everything is in line. I don't take on any more cases. I just make sure everyone is doing what they're supposed to be doing, but I'm okay with it because it allows me to take care of my girls. Zoey still works when she wants, taking on jobs that interest her when it suits her. We've both got enough money to not have to worry about it, so we get to spend time with our daughter and each other.

Amelia makes a humming noise like she likes it, and Zoey looks at her skeptically. After a second, she picks up her fork and tries it, too, making the same exact face as Amelia. I can hardly hold back my eye roll. They're so alike. God help me, I love the two of them more than life itself. I don't know how my heart can possibly have any more room for love, but seeing Zoey round with our next little girl, I'm already head over heels for her, too.

After everything settled down from the stalker drama, we got married in a double ceremony just like Zoey wanted. It was a big wedding and lots of fun, but in the end I was just happy to have my cupcake beside me.

Zoey got pregnant about a minute after we met, and I couldn't have been happier with our little girl. We decided to wait a while after Amelia was born, thinking we needed some time to adjust to kids. After she was a couple years old, we started trying again and finally got pregnant with our baby girl on the way now. I should be terrified of having another girl, but I couldn't be more excited. I hope our new bundle of love is just like her mama, too.

Reaching over, I rub her belly and then look up into Zoey's eyes.

"Thank you," I whisper, and she looks at me, cocking her head to the side.

"For what?"

"For this." I look between her and Amelia. "For everything. I'm a lucky bastard."

"Ooooooh! Daddy said a bad word."

"She's right, you did," Zoey agrees, and I just smile at them.

Life is too damn good.

Fifteen years later...

"Oh, fuck!"

"Shhh. The girls are downstairs. They'll hear us."

"Oh, fuck," Zoey whispers.

I smile against her pussy and then start licking her again. I get lost in her sweet honeysuckle, licking her in long thick strokes just the way she likes it. She lies back on the bed, grabbing the pillow and putting it over her face. She's trying to be good, but I really am torturing her.

Our oldest, Amelia, is home from college and took her sister, Brock to the movies with her. I guess they got back early, because we heard them downstairs just as things were getting hot. I jumped up and locked the door but refused to let Zoey go. They'll be fine without us for a while.

Zoey makes mumbled noises into the pillow as I eat her pussy. I bring up two fingers and push them through her wet folds, and then deep inside her. She moans and clenches around them, and my dick throbs in response.

Sucking her clit into my mouth, I graze it with my teeth, making her legs shake with need. I curl my fingers up, hitting her G spot, and start to work them in and out of her. Flicking her little nub with the end of my tongue is enough to send her over the edge.

Her legs tense, and her back bows off the bed while she screams my name into the pillow. Even after all these years, I haven't gotten tired of that sound. There's never been another woman who's caught my attention or made me question for one second my devotion to Zoey. She's the only woman who ever saw me for who I am, and she's my reason for breathing.

Kissing the inside of her thighs, I rub my nose against her, just letting her ride her orgasm to its end while I pet her and give her little pecks of love.

"Mom?" I hear Brock's voice and then a knock on the door.

Zoey giggles into the pillow, and I turn my head back toward the door. "Go away!" I yell as I climb up the bed and on top of Zoey. She's shaking with laughter, and I move the pillow to whisper in her ear. "That was your fault this time."

"What are you guys doing in there?" Amelia shouts from the other side of the door, and I roll my eyes.

"There's money in my purse. Go get ice cream. Leave us alone!" Zoey yells, and then I hear the girls head back downstairs.

It's all I can do not to fall on top of her laughing,

but then she reaches between us and grabs my cock. All the laughter leaves me, and my desire shoots to the forefront.

"Orgasms, Hart. I want all of them."

She guides my cock to her opening, and I thrust in the rest of the way. "Whatever you want, cupcake," I grunt out as I start to move inside of her.

Leaning down, I suck on her hard nipple, needing something in my mouth to keep me quiet. It's been almost two decades since I first got inside her, and her pussy still grips me tighter than anything I've ever known. Her warm, wet heat sucks me inside her, and I have to bite down on her nipple to keep from cumming. Her hands go to my back, her nails digging in, and I feel her clenches start again.

"Drake," she moans, and she cums all over my cock.

There's nothing sweeter than the feel of her pleasure on me and under me. Getting Zoey off is what gets me off, and I follow her into sweet oblivion.

When we both catch our breath and I take my mouth off of her nipple, I look up into her eyes.

She reaches between us, rubbing her hand over the space on my chest where her pink cupcake is tattooed. All these years later, she still looks at it and smiles. Just like the first time she saw it. I even had two more little cupcakes tattooed beside it to represent my little girls.

Seeing her like this is what makes my life worth living.

There are little fine lines around her beautiful eyes as she smiles up at me, and I can't help but fall in love with each of them. Each one represents a smile she's given me or our girls. Each crease is a memory I've shared with her, and each one I cherish.

"What?" she asks, smiling up at me.

"I love you, cupcake."

"I love you, too, Drake. And I want another orgasm."

Elle and Daniel aka Pink

It's been fifteen years since the day I first saw Elle, and I never get tired of looking at her. She's in the kitchen setting out lunches and making sure everything is ready to go for in the morning. I walk up behind her. Wrapping my arms around her waist, I bury my face in her neck and just breathe her in.

"Don't start something you can't finish," she laughs as she rubs her ass against me.

"Who's saying I won't finish it?" She turns in my arms and gives me a kiss as she reaches down and grabs my ass. Leaning my forehead against hers, I think about all that we've shared these past years.

We've had six kids together—three boys and three girls—and Elle runs this place like a drill sergeant. I'm so proud of the mother she's become and of how amazing she is, but I still like to get her riled up. She keeps us all organized, and I make sure to mess her schedule up every now and then to remind her that chaos can be fun, too. She gets bent out of shape, but getting her steamed up is half the fun.

"I've got to finish this and then set the coffee,

fold the laundry, and get the hockey bags ready for practice after school. Then I need to—"

I put my finger over her lips and give her a look.

"Don't give me that look, Pink," she says, pushing my hand away. "I have too much to do."

"Not tonight," I say, and raise an eyebrow. "I've already done all that shit. It may not be the way you like it, but it's done."

She starts to talk, but I put my hand in her hair and grip a handful of it.

"I'm taking you upstairs. I want you to take your clothes off and get in the bath I ran for you. I'm going fuck you in it and then rub your feet."

I feel her melt in my arms, and I know I've got her. I've always known Elle to be highly strung, but all she needs is a little control taken away and she's like warm butter for me.

She likes everything done a certain way, but her dominance can only last so long. We both know who's really in charge, and most of the time she needs reminding.

I reach down and grab her ass with both hands, picking her up. Her arms and legs go around me, and I carry her up the stairs to our bedroom. I kick the door closed behind us and lock it before taking her to the master bath.

I strip down and get in the tub, which is more than big enough for the two of us, and lean back to watch her take her clothes off. She knows what I want, and I wait for it.

Slowly, she starts to move her hips as she strips out of her clothes. I've got soft music playing, and she takes her time, letting me see everything that's mine.

Once she's undressed, she walks over and gets in the tub, standing up over me. Taking her hands, I pull her down so she's straddling my hips. She reaches down between us, holding my cock as she lowers herself onto it.

When she's fully seated on me, I grab her hips and work them up and down.

"Say it, *Prinzessin*."

Elle knows I want to hear her words of love when I'm inside her. Nothing turns me on more than when I've got my cock in her and she tells me she loves me. It's the most perfect thing in the world, and every time we connect, I need it to leave her lips.

"I love you, Daniel. Only you."

All these years later and I still get off hearing that I'm the only one she wants. That there have been no others before me.

"I love you, too, Elle."

The candles flicker in the bathroom and reflect the shadows of our bodies becoming one. We make love, and I give her the foot rub I promised, all while she tells me about her day. I refill the tub with warm water countless times because I'm not ready for tonight to end.

Some days are hectic, especially with six kids, so nights like these are savored. When I finally pull her from the tub, she's putty in my arms as I take her to bed and kiss every inch of her.

Elle needed me to break down her walls and help her see the beauty in chaos. Every day we are together is another chance for me to show her just how perfect our love is. And tonight, as she drifts to sleep in my arms, I kiss her forehead and thank my lucky stars she chose me.

snow *and* mistletoe

CHAPTER ONE

noelle

"'Please," she begged. "I need to feel you inside me now. It's been too long." Annabelle pleaded with Sam before taking matters into her own hands, grabbing his hard cock and guiding it to her wet pussy. Wanting to make them whole once again, to never be apart from the only man she'd ever loved. Would ever love.

"I'll give you what you want. Just give me what I want," Sam demanded, pulling back just a little from her, the head of his cock barely touching her opening. She knew what he wanted, and she was sick of fighting these feelings. She'd find a way to make them work, no matter how different their worlds were.

"I love you. Only you." She gave him the words he wanted because they were true. She knew it down to her soul.

Samuel thrust home into her welcoming body, his hard cock just as hungry for her as he was."

The heavy breathing through the phone pulls me from my narration "Mr. Lockwood, are you okay?"

"Alex," he grunts, sounding irritated with me. "Say it."

"Alex," I whisper. He's been correcting me for months now, but for some reason I always still say 'Mr. Lockwood.' It reminds me of who he is—that he isn't a friend I'm talking to on the phone. He's a client and nothing more, no matter what my late-night fantasies tell me.

I hear a grunt, then the line goes quiet. I wonder if he's mad at me, and I inwardly curse myself. I had steady work before I started narrating books for his company, All for You, but with him offering me more and more projects, he's been my only client for well over two months now. It sounds silly, and I'm sure I can get more projects elsewhere, but I like working for him. He handles things a little differently than most clients I work with, but I like his way. Seems I like a lot of things about Alex, despite knowing very little about him.

The silence hangs in the air as I wait for him to speak again. His words do things to me. Things they shouldn't. I've somehow latched myself onto him recently. Waiting for our daily calls has now become a little bit of an obsession, one I'm sure my mother would tell me was just as unhealthy as my lack of a social life.

"Hmm," I mumble, trying to break the uncomfortable silence. I can't bear the tension, but all

I hear is his heavy breathing, something that reminds me of the many erotica books I've read. The hero would breathlessly pant into the heroine's ear after a hard round of sex. It's a sound I've never actually heard myself, but I find myself imagining what it would be like if Alex made the sound in my ear, his body on top of me.

"I think that's enough for today," he finally says, his deep voice rolling over my skin like a warm rough caress, like it always does when he speaks to me. If anyone one should be narrating a book, it's Alex. He has a voice like I've never heard before, and I've heard many in my line of work. Voices that are supposed to be the best aren't anything special compared to his.

"Okay, Mis— Alex," I correct myself quickly, once again making myself look like an incompetent fool who can't remember anything. "I'll have the Scott book sent over this afternoon. Just a few more touches and it will be finished. Then I'll start on this new one, if you liked the sample I just did."

Alex likes to do the samples over the phone and also likes to check in daily on my project status, something that's not normal with audio work. Almost everything could be done over email, but Alex says he likes to do it this way. For what he's paying me to voice audiobooks, I'm happy to jump through hoops for the projects. Okay, that's only partially true. I would jump through the hoops, but our phone calls mean more to me than just work.

Sometimes our calls dip into personal life, mainly about me and my life. Every now and then, I find myself rambling on, and he just listens. Maybe he's really polite and feels sorry for me for having to carry on conversations with someone who is virtually a stranger. Though he doesn't feel like a stranger anymore.

"That sounds perfect. I have a lot going on tomorrow, so I want this taken care of tonight and off both our to-do lists," he says, slipping back into business talk. It's crazy how he does that. Sometimes I wonder if maybe he has a crazy sex life, because my narrations always seem to run on the dirty side and they never affect him.

I usually end up in a pile of goo when we we're done, with hard nipples and wet panties. We'd hang up and I'd have my hand down my pants before the line even cleared. It wasn't narrating the books that turned me on. I've been doing romance narrations for years. Normally I did them alone so no one would hear. But somehow, reading aloud to Alex has me beyond turned on. It could be that the pieces he selects for samples are always the dirtiest parts, or it could just be him.

I told myself it was because Alex was playing with me. I thought maybe he even had a little crush on me like I did him, but after time went on, he never seemed affected. He never tried to be more friendly to me like I was with him, and after a while I thought maybe I made it up in my head. My mother always told me I live too much inside myself, and it seemed to have happened again. I'd built something up in my mind that wasn't really there. Worse, the thought of not having this interaction anymore was terrifying in some weird way.

"Okay. I'll send the file right over." I try to keep my tone just as causal as his, but I'm still chewing on the fact that he has a lot going on tomorrow. It's Christmas, so I should expect him to be busy. All I have planned is a TV dinner and Netflix.

"Have a merry Christmas, Noelle."

"You too, Alex." I hit End on the call, promptly wanting to disconnect from him. I drop the phone onto my desk and bring up my emails. I want to go ahead and send the file, but my internet won't connect. After restarting the modem and my laptop, I make my way over to the window while everything reboots.

It really is a perfect Christmas Eve. Snow has already begun to fall, and the Christmas lights on my tree behind me reflect in the window. It's as if they're mocking me. My house is decorated like I'm hosting a Christmas party tomorrow. There isn't a spot that isn't covered in some kind of Christmas decoration. Why I do this to myself, I have no idea.

I'm an introvert and always have been. I made a couple of friends in college, always preferring to have my nose deep in a book. But since then they've dropped off one by one, slowly losing contact over time. No one wants to be friends with the girl who rarely leaves the house.

Who knows where my parents are this time of year. No one likes to travel more than they do. I still have no idea how I came from such social butterflies. I like things small and intimate, and I always wanted to spend a Christmas like that with my parents. When I was a kid, my mom would go all out, kind of like I did in my own home, but she always filled the day with people I hardly knew.

It's almost laughable now. I hate how she'd do that, but now here I am in a house all made up for Christmas and not one soul to spend it with. I'm not sure which is worse.

My mind wanders back to Alex, wondering what his plans might be. Would he have a special person to spend his Christmas with? The thought sends an irrational surge of jealously through me.

Maybe I can come up with a reason to get in touch with him, or just call to wish him a merry Christmas. I chastise myself for the silly idea. Considering how fast he got off the phone moments ago, he probably has plans tonight.

Growling at myself, I pull my hair from my ponytail to relieve some of the tension I'm feeling.

Pull it together, I tell myself. I'll finish this project for Alex, get into my Christmas pajamas, eat those cookies I spent all day baking and decorating, and watch my favorite holiday movies. I will not let myself have a pity party.

CHAPTER TWO

alex

I hang up the phone and lean back in my chair, sighing. I close my eyes and let the sound of my name coming out of her sinful mouth roll around in my head. *"Alex, Alex, Alex."* I envision her saying it over and over as I drive into her. The thought has me ready to cum all over again, and I reach over to grab a box of tissues to clean up the cum from the orgasm I already had.

After the first time I heard her voice and had her read a scene for me, I started keeping a box of tissues close by. With every syllable out of her mouth, I got harder and harder until I finally had to mute the phone and rub one out. I couldn't stand it, her voice driving me beyond wild. I've never reacted to a voice the way I do to Noelle's and the more I hear her, the more I want her.

I've been living in this cabin in Montana for a few years now. I started my company, All for You, a few years ago, after the accident.

The accident.

I worked as a publicist for a publishing house in New York, working with authors and agents. One day when I was on my way home from work, I was crossing the street in front of my apartment and was hit by a car. The driver never saw me, and all my doctors said I was lucky to be alive. The accident left a good portion of my body scarred up, including one side of my face. It took months to heal, and afterwards, I felt cramped and claustrophobic in the big city. The scarring was too much for me to handle out in public, and I needed to get away from the noise.

I wanted to work from home, and audiobooks were something I'd helped a few authors with before. So I started my company to help my clients find the perfect fit for their audiobooks, and before I knew it I had a long list of people needing my services.

I bought my cabin out in Montana a few years before the accident, visiting as often as I could but not as much as I liked. When I was well enough, I decided to ditch the Big Apple and go live the way I wanted to. My parents and sister still live back in New York, loving the bustling metropolis. At first they were sad I was leaving, but I think they understood my need for isolation. I enjoyed being on my own a lot before, but after the accident, it was difficult to be in public. But technology is great, and it allows me to keep in touch with them. I usually visit them about once a year, and it's enough for me. We all call and email, but I like my solitude. They ask me every year about coming home for Christmas, and I have a couple of times. But every year I've gone home, all I can think about is getting back to my quiet cabin in the woods.

I've grown my business, and now I have a wait list of authors wanting my services. I take one of their books and help match them up with the perfect reader. Normally, I tweak them when necessary, but otherwise, I make the match for them and move on to the next.

Until Noelle.

The first time I heard her audition, I was looking for a female voice for one of my clients' spy thrillers. She submitted her resumé, and I sent her a voice sample, wanting to see if she would fit his needs. The sample I sent her was completely tame, just a chapter about the heroine's research on the case. But every tone in Noelle's voice made my cock hard. It sounded as if she was speaking directly to me, and it sent vibrations through my bones. The most unassuming chapter she could have ever read came alive with emotions I never knew were possible.

That day I hired her on and started using her for all the female parts I needed. After a while, though, I needed more. I had to have something deeper from Noelle.

I started scouring romance authors who had audiobook needs, and I picked up a few clients. I would pore over books until I found the sweetest, dirtiest ones possible and save specific sections for her to read. I turned all my attention to this side of the business, focusing on Noelle and her voice work in romance. My own selfish needs taking over, and consuming me.

I would record her reading to me over the phone so I could play it back again every night before I went to bed, always being too worked up during her live reading to fully take in every detail of her words. I find that when I play it back at night, I can hear so much more than what she's reading; I can hear her sensual melody as I fall asleep.

After the first time I had her read a romance book, I found myself unable to send it to the author. Instead, I used someone else for the audiobook. I couldn't bring myself to share Noelle's voice with anyone else, and I know that was crazy. I've been paying her to record audiobooks for months, but I've never sent any of her work to an author, instead paying her out of my own money and using another reader for the job.

I'd made plenty of money in my life so that if I never worked again and only paid Noelle to read to me, she could until the end of time and I wouldn't be hurting for the cash. As it is, I've pretty much stopped taking all jobs unless they revolve around Noelle and her voice.

The best part of my day is picking up the phone to call her. I get hard before I even dial the number. She sent her picture with her online resumé, and I'm just sad enough to admit that I printed it out and it's on my desk. I look at it as she reads to me over the phone and I slowly stroke myself.

Even after she's finished getting me off, and I sit there, trying to catch my breath, just hearing her go on about her day and life makes me the happiest man in the world. What I wouldn't give to touch her.

Shutting down that thought, I stand up and throw the cum-covered tissue away and button up my jeans. I walk out back, grabbing the axe on the back porch, and go to chop some wood. It will help keep my mind busy while I try not to think about things I can't have.

Noelle is utterly beautiful, with big brown eyes and wavy light-brown hair. Her full lips are smiling in the photo she sent me, her cheeks rosy with life. From what she's told me, she only lives about three hours from where I am, but she doesn't know that. She just happened to tell me the town she was living in one day, and I looked it up. I also know she's single, and I clench my jaw at the thought. How could anyone see her and hear her voice and not want to scoop her up? At the same time, the thought makes me angry as I picture someone else getting to have her.

Bringing the axe down on the wood, I watch as it splinters in two. I let out a long sigh and wish for the millionth time that I'd seen that car coming. If I was whole and man enough to sweep Noelle off her feet, I'd get in my truck and drive the three hours to knock on her door and ask her out on a date. She's so perfect, and she deserves the best. Not half a man who has little kids staring at him at the supermarket.

I guess I'll just have to settle for jerking off to her voice for the rest of my life. It's not exactly what I want, but a part of her is better than nothing. And if she never finds out, then what's the harm? I can have my own perfect fantasy in my head, where she's mine and I'm whole.

Ignoring my loneliness, I undertake the task of chopping more wood, adding to the mountain I already have. Winter in Montana is no joke, but my house is pretty well stocked. I've got power from the town that's pretty close and a fireplace in my bedroom, just in case. There's also a wood stove in the kitchen for cooking when I feel the need, but as long as I've got power, I don't use it. The cabin is pretty roomy for one person, with a living room and kitchen all together. There's a master bedroom downstairs with an attached bath and two rooms upstairs with a bathroom in between. I use one for my office and one is a spare bedroom, though I've never needed it. The place was furnished when I bought it, and I just left it alone.

The snow starts to come down heavier, which is expected this time of year. I haul my freshly cut wood onto the porch and make my way inside. After removing my heavy coat and boots, I go to my bedroom and turn on my laptop.

Lying down in the middle of the bed, I hit play, and Noelle's voice fills the room. I reach one hand down the front of my jeans, stroking my hard cock while she tells me all about the things I want to do to her.

CHAPTER THREE

noelle

Smacking the modem again, I know my efforts are fruitless. I've reset the stupid thing four times now and nothing has gotten it to work. My only other option was smacking it, and that doesn't seem to be working either. Glancing out the window, I can see the snow starting to come down a little harder, but not enough to make me think it would cause internet issues.

"Damn it." I smack the modem again, saying a silent prayer, and all the lights go out on it. Dead. Like my contract with 'All for You.' The thought makes my stomach turn sour. No more Alex. Maybe he won't fire me, but maybe he will. He told me he wanted this today. I glance at the clock and see it's already five p. m. on Christmas Eve. Everything is closed. There's no way I can even pack up and go to a local coffee shop to use their Wi-Fi to send the file.

My options are running out. No, not running out. I have none. Zero. I'm screwed. Maybe I can call and explain and make him understand. I decide to give it a shot. I call Alex. It's something I've never done before because he always calls me. The phone rings six times before going to voice mail, making me wonder what he's doing. I roll my eyes, thinking it's none of my business.

He's probably sitting in front of a fire with his family or girlfriend, eating cookies and having an oh-so-perfect Christmas. I'm sure it's like one of those sappy romance novels I've narrated before.

Plopping down on the couch, I begin mourning the loss of the best contract I've ever had. Screw that. It isn't the job I'm sad about losing, it's him. He seems to have this weird hold on me. How have I latched myself onto someone I barely know? Someone who never shares anything personal about themselves, even when I try to pull things from him. Sometimes I feel like it is there on the tip of his tongue, but it just never comes.

When my phone rings, it makes me jump off the couch and hurriedly pick it up without looking to see who it is.

"Alex?" I say into the phone, hating the way my voice comes out all breathy like I just ran a mile.

"Who's Alex?" my mom chirps into the phone, making me drop back down onto the couch.

"No one, Mom." The lie easily rolls off my tongue. I don't want to get into it with her about an imaginary relationship with a man who is essentially my boss. She'd ask me what he looks like, how often we went out, on and on. All things I couldn't answer, and that's when she'd really start in on me about being more social and how I should maybe talk to a head shrinker to see what was wrong with me.

Nothing is wrong with me. I'm just a homebody. I haven't found a person who wants to be a homebody with me yet. The future isn't looking too great on me finding one either. Not when I'm daydreaming about a man I've never even met.

"Doesn't sound like nobody," she says, poking again, but I know she means well. I may not click with my mom and dad, but they love me.

"Just a client. I'm working on a last-minute project, and I need to talk to him, but can't get a hold of him." I give her a little honest information, hoping it will end the questions and we can change the topic. I reach for one of the cookies on the plate I'd set out on the coffee table and take a bite. The sweetness does nothing to make me feel better. I'm going to need cake for that.

"He's probably with his family like you should be. Is this project the reason you decided not to join us? I bet you took on a job just so you couldn't come this Christmas." The huff in her voice is one I'm all too used to. It works better on my father than me.

"I wasn't invited." I don't mention that I don't even know where they are right now. Since I moved out, my mom stopped with the big parties and moved on to spending Christmas in random places in fancy hotels.

"You're always invited." The hurt in her voice makes me feel instantly guilty. I know I'm always invited, but it still burned I didn't get a call or something. "Didn't you get my card?"

"Ahh," I muddle, dropping the cookie back onto the plate and heading towards the front door entryway. I keep a basket on the table there and always throw my mail in it. I'm looking at the pile as my mom tells me what they're doing and how she wishes I was there.

I never go through that basket until it's practically overflowing. Most of it is normally junk anyway. All my bills are paid online. Who needs mail? If it doesn't come in an Amazon box, I'm not interested. It goes into the mail basket. I go through it about once a month when it starts to overfill and spill onto the table, leaving me no choice.

Digging through it, I search for cards, pulling out a sad total of three, while my mom continues to rattle on about Paris. Most people get tons of cards that they line their fireplaces with or cover their refrigerator with. The first card is a generic one from my dentist, but the second one stops me dead. His name is handwritten on the top-left corner. No stupid stamp or printed-out label. Alex Lockwood.

Even his writing is sexy and masculine, making me warm all over.

"Mom, I've got to go. Merry Christmas. I love you." I rudely cut my mom off as she lists off the people she and Dad are seeing tomorrow. I didn't have a clue who any of them were anyway, and I've got more pressing matters on my hands.

I open the card, careful not to rip the envelope too much, wanting to keep it as perfect as possible. The front of the card shows a pretty snow scene—a simple cabin with snow falling all around it. Above the picture-perfect wintery image is *Merry Christmas*, written in a rustic font.

Printed inside is a simple *May all your Christmas wishes come true*. But below that, written in that distinctive handwriting, is what grabs my attention.

To the sweetest voice I know.

xoxo

Alex.

My heart starts to race at the simple words, and I trace my finger over the *xoxo*. Maybe he was just being nice, but was it normal to tell a woman she has the sweetest voice he knew and add hugs and kisses, or was he flirting with me? Or am I once again making too much out of this? There were just as many hugs as there were kisses. Of course he'd comment on my voice. That's what I do for him, after all. Maybe he did cards for everyone at work, like the stupid dentist card I got. For all I know, he has a secretary who does them and he just signs them.

Flipping the envelope over, I see an address that doesn't match his company headquarters. I know because it's stamped on the contracts I sign with every new book I take on. It's odd, because this one is much closer to me. This address is only three hours from my house. I know the town and have been there a few times. I remember it being small and quaint when I went there to look at antiques one afternoon.

I make a snap judgment. The card said *May all*

your Christmas wishes come true, and this year my wish is not to lose Alex from my life. Even if it means keeping me firmly in the role of his employee, I'll take it. I'm doing what I have to do, and I'm going to his house. Loading up the audio tracks to a USB drive, I figure I can just take it to him. Then he'll have his work, and I'll know without a shadow of a doubt that I won't be getting fired.

I know I might be crazy, but the thought of not having my daily calls with Alex is shattering. They're something I'm not ready to let go of, even if my obsession has gotten a bit unhealthy. Glancing out the window, I can see the snow has picked up a little more. By the time I get out there, it will be really late. I should pack a bag and maybe stay at a local motel or something. If the snow keeps falling like it is, it probably won't be safe to drive back tonight.

I rush to my bedroom and hurriedly get a bag together, stopping in front of the mirror to look at myself. I'm going to see him. I'm actually going to be face to face with Alex. I smooth down my brown hair, knowing I don't have much time to do anything to it. I'm in leggings and a silly Christmas sweater that hugs my body a little tighter than it did a few years ago. It's festooned with blinking lights you can turn on.

Doesn't matter, I tell myself, grabbing my bag. I slip on some boots, a heavy winter coat, and a stocking cap. I grab the USB drive and my laptop, dropping them into the bag as well. I head out to my Jeep and program the address into my navigation. I hit the garage button, pull out of my driveway, and sit there while I watch it close.

An hour into the drive, my mind starts to get the best of me. What will happen when I get there? Will he be angry that I interrupted his Christmas? Or will he be happy he got the files he needed, and maybe invite me in? But when my mind goes to him maybe spending the holiday with a woman, I know I have to focus my thoughts somewhere else.

Grabbing my phone, I hit my Audible app and bring up my downloaded books. I hit one of the ones I recorded for Alex. I purchased the audiobook when it went live the other day. I want to listen to the story and get my mind off things, but as the first words are read, what fills my ears makes my stomach knot.

CHAPTER FOUR

alex

After I jerk off twice while listening to Noelle's voice, I decide to get out of bed and get something to eat. I could stay in bed all day listening to her and touching myself, but it seems kind of sad to spend my Christmas Eve that way.

I put on some long sweats and a thermal shirt, choosing to dress for bed since it's getting late. Going over to my stereo, I play the Peanuts Christmas album. I know that if I put on another audio of Noelle, I'll just end up back in bed, stroking myself to her voice. I go to my refrigerator, trying to figure out what I want. I have a big dinner planned for myself tomorrow because I enjoy cooking, and I wanted to do something a little special for Christmas Day. Nothing in my small town would be open anyway, so spending the day reading and eating indoors is on the agenda.

Looking out the kitchen window, I see the sun setting and the snow is coming down heavily. I'm wondering if the power will even hold out for me to cook. Good thing I've got plenty of wood and a fireplace with a stovetop to cook on. I prepared for a worst-case scenario, knowing how bad the weather can be this time of year. Two years ago I got snowed in for over a week and had to hike it into town for supplies. I'm not planning on doing that again. Ever.

As I pull out stuff to make sandwiches, I think about how I should get a cat or a dog. Something to keep me company during times like this. I enjoy my solitude and being away from the world, but at times it gets really lonely. When I do go into town, I don't talk to people unless I have to, and I try to cover up my scars as much as possible. I don't like people looking at me and wondering what happened. Or worse, feeling sorry for me.

Shaking off that thought, I go back to making myself something to eat. When that's done, I go over to the living room and sit down in front of the fire. I stare at the flames, thinking about Noelle and wondering what she's doing right now.

She's probably with her family like every other normal person. Enjoying her Christmas Eve with loved ones, or maybe going out with friends. Maybe she'll meet someone while she's out, someone who can be seen in public with her and who won't feel the need to hide himself.

I think about what it would be like to spend

Christmas with Noelle. If I was whole, and she was mine, I think I'd overdose on Christmas cheer. I'd want to spend all day in bed, cuddled up naked and keeping warm. I'd want to make love to her over and over, only letting her out of bed to make cookies with me and to open presents by the fire. Naked, of course. I'd want to taste every inch of her curvy body, eating her pussy in front of the fireplace. I'd want to fuck her over the kitchen counter so she was covered with flour and sprinkles. I'd drag her outside to make snow angels until she was frozen, and then I'd drag her into the tub and give her a bath until she was warm. I'd hold her close to me that night and whisper in her ear how much I lov—.

"Come on, Alex," I tell myself, trying to shake off the fantasy. It's not real, and it never will be. What I have is in my head and nothing more. Thinking I need something to lift my spirits, I walk to my bedroom and grab Noelle's recording along with my cell phone. I glance down at it as I walk back to the kitchen and freeze when I see a missed call from her.

I don't think twice as I call her back immediately, wondering how I could have missed it. Oh yeah, I was busy jerking off a couple of times listening to her read dirty books out loud. Jesus, Alex, could you be more fucking lame?

After just one ring, the call disconnects, and I look down at my phone, seeing I've got service. I try again and again I get disconnected after one ring. I try five more times and nothing happens. I get a sick feeling in my stomach. What if something happened? What if something went wrong?

I check the time she called and see that it was over three hours ago. I start to worry. Who can I call and talk to? How can I find out if she's okay? Did I get a family member contact when I had her sign her contract? God, why didn't I think of something like this happening?

I start to pace the living room, thinking of how to get in touch with her, when I see headlights flash across the room.

"What the fuck?"

Who could possibly be coming to my house? I've never had anyone come here, and my family wouldn't just show up without telling me. Maybe they're lost. But my driveway is three miles long. Whoever comes down the road this far knows where they're going.

I go to the hall closet and grab the bat I keep in there. I have a hunting rifle, but it's in the back of the house and not loaded. Probably not the best place for it in this situation, but I've never needed it before.

I pull on my boots as fast as I can. I throw on my coat and walk towards the front door. I see the Jeep turn into the driveway and park just as I walk off the porch and down the front steps. I stand there for half a second, holding the bat, and wait to see who gets out. The snow is really pouring down now, and even a few feet away from the car, it's hard to make out what's happening.

When a small woman in a big coat and stocking cap rounds the back of the Jeep, I squint as I try to make out who it is. She stops short when she sees me with a bat in my hand, and it's then I realize I don't have anything on to cover my face. I'm not wearing a hat or scarf, and my scars must frighten her.

I can't see her eyes very well with all the snow that's coming down, but I lower the bat a little, thinking she must need some kind of help to come out this far.

"Alex?"

The one word nearly knocks me over on my ass. I let the bat drop into the snow and I turn around, quickly giving Noelle my back. I can't let her see me. How did she even get here?

"What are doing here, Noelle?" I can hear the cold callous sound in my voice, but I can't stop it.

"I...I had a problem with my internet. I needed to get the book back to you today."

Her warm voice is silky, like melted caramel rolling over my tense shoulders and penetrating my heart. My cock responds to her like it always does, going rock hard even in this frosty weather.

"You shouldn't be out in this weather." All I can think about is how dangerous it was for her to come here.

There's silence for half a second, and then I hear her feet shuffle slightly. "You're right. It was a real bitch getting here. I'm sorry. I tried to call, but I didn't want to miss a deadline." I hear her nervous laughter and have to rein myself in from going to comfort her. "I'm sorry, we can do this another time. I'll just make my way back to town and try to call you later."

"*No!*" I don't turn around, but the word echoes through the forest, silencing her.

I never dreamed she would be here, and now that

she is, I can't stand the thought of her leaving. It's too dangerous for her to drive anywhere else, not that I would let her anyway.

"The weather is getting worse. You can't drive in this."

"I'm sorry, Alex. I just didn't want to lose my job. I'm sorry I disturbed you on Christmas Eve. I saw the town just a few miles back. I can go to the motel there, and maybe we can talk after the holiday."

"Stay!" I turn around quickly, throwing out the word before I have a chance to pull it back. I look away, not making eye contact and trying to keep my head turned so the worst of my scars aren't facing her. "The motel is full. You can stay with me. I have a room." I have no idea if the motel is full or not. I just don't want Noelle to leave.

"I can't put you out like that, Alex. I'm really sorry—"

"Just come inside. It's freezing." I wait for a second, and I see her turn to her Jeep and grab a bag out of the back. "You can stay the night. In the morning I can take you to the motel in town."

"Thank you," she whispers, and I turn to walk into the house. When I hear sound of her footsteps following behind me, I release a breath I didn't know I was holding. How bad can this be? I can stay clear of her for one night. I can do this.

Right?

CHAPTER FIVE

noelle

I quickly grab my bag from the passenger seat and follow in his wake, my heart pounding.

"You cold?" he asks, stomping his boots and shaking the snow from them on the front door mat. I follow his lead, doing the same, not wanting to track snow into his cabin.

"Ah, yeah." It's freezing out, but the wind seems to have more of a bite out here than it did in town. The cold cuts right through you out here. I could feel it rattle my car the further I got from the city.

I follow him into the cabin before pulling off my boots and placing them by the door. He does the same, keeping his back to me as he does it. I can't help but stare at his broad shoulders. I thought he'd be a big guy as he has such a deep voice, but he's even bigger than I imagined. He's over six feet, probably coming in a good foot over my five two stature. Most people have a lot of inches on me, but he has more than most.

He turns his head a little, glancing over his shoulder at me. One deep blue eye meets mine. Loose, charcoal hair falls over his face, like he's in need of a slight trim, and it blocks my view of his face. I'm dying to see it. It looked like he had a scar running down his forehead to his cheekbone when I saw him first. But with the dim light in the cabin and his hair blocking my view, it's hard to tell.

He reminds me of one of the old romance heroes I read about in my mom's old trashy novels. Everyone in the books seemed to carry a brooding aura around them. And were always blessed with dark hair and sharp blue eyes. It never failed time and time again that the heroes would be described that way. Whenever I'd pick up another one of her books, I could almost predict when it was going to say it, and now I seem to be standing mere feet from one, ripped straight from the pages.

I push the silly thought from my head because I'm once again living in my own fantasy, making real something that isn't. I take a step toward him, unable to stop myself from reaching to move the hair out of his face. I don't know what's making me so bold, but I regret it instantly when he turns his head, giving me his broad back again, mumbling something I can't quite catch.

It is almost like he doesn't want to look at me or something. The thought sends a cold chill down my spine that has nothing to do with the weather. In fact, it's kind of warm in here with me still all bundled up and a fire blazing at the far wall. I'm guessing this is the living room as a Christmas tree sits in the corner, colored lights dancing across it.

I've been dying to know what he looks like. I wanted to match a face to the man who's been starring in my fantasies for the past few months. When I got out of the car, he took my breath away. I couldn't even see him fully and I was entranced, just from being near him.

Being so close after wanting him for so long, I found his words were hard and nothing like I'd thought they'd be. At times he could be firm with me, like when I called him by his last name, or when it took me a few rings to pick up the phone when he called, but what happened outside was confusing and unsettling. It was like he wanted me to get the hell out of here. Only he didn't really want me to leave at the same time.

"I...uh..." I say, trying to break the silence between us for the second time today. I'm totally getting fired. Hell, I kinda knew that when I popped on my audiobook and my voice wasn't even on it. As much as I want to ask, I don't feel like poking the bear he seems to have turned into.

I knew he was the silent broody type, but I didn't think he bit. Now I'm not so sure. He could rip my heart to shreds with a few harsh words. Maybe this is why I spend so much time with my head in the clouds and my nose in books, dreaming in my own little world. This real-life romance shit is hard and scary.

"Follow me. I'll show you where you can put your stuff," he says without looking at me as he heads towards a hallway. It's as if he wants to shove me into a room as quickly as possible. He won't even look at me, and a lump starts to form in my throat. Forget it. I can't do this.

"Maybe I should just..." I turn to grab the door handle, but I remember I don't have my shoes on so I can't make as quick of an escape as I'd like. Before I can turn to grab my shoes, big arms shoot out on either side of me, landing on the door. His warm body presses into mine.

"Don't go." His words are soft this time, and they tickle my ear. He doesn't move, and I can't seem to form any words with him pressed up against me like this. "Just let me show you to your room. You can take a warm bath if you like."

"Okay." The fight leaves my body at his deep, sensual voice. My answer comes out breathy, and it takes every muscle in my body to stop myself from leaning into him. I want to rub against him like a cat in heat. I've never done anything wanton in my life, but Alex makes me do a lot of things I've never done before. Like drive three hours in a snowstorm, pretending it was all about saving my job, when really I'm being a low-key stalker.

Maybe I can just say I'm cold or something if I rub against him. Oh my God, I'm totally trying to cop a feel! My cheeks burn with embarrassment at my own thoughts, but Alex still makes no move to release me. I can't move until he drops the big arms that are caging me. God, how I wish I was facing the other way and staring into his dark blue eyes. I was so sure they would be brown when I pictured him, but my thoughts didn't do those eyes justice.

"Don't try to leave again." The firmness in his voice is one I know all too well. I am about to tell him I'll do whatever I want, but feeling him pressed against me banishes any thoughts I have of leaving this cabin. "It's dark, the snow is falling thick, and the coyotes will be out."

With that caution, the warmth of his body leaves mine, and I miss it instantly. Sadly, I think I could have stood like that all night and been utterly content. I turn, following him down the long hallway. The cabin is cute. It's hard to make out much with so few lights on, but all the walls and floors are wooden. It's rustic and homely and utterly perfect. The place looks like it was plucked right out of some catalogue. It would be the perfect place to spend Christmas.

The thought reminds me that it's Christmas Eve. I haven't heard anyone else, but I feel bad, not only for intruding but for possibly putting someone out of a bedroom. "Are we alone?" I'm prying for information, but I'm wondering if a girlfriend or someone like that is going to pop up.

"I'm always alone." That makes me happy until the words really sink it.

He takes me upstairs, and we pass one door before we stop outside another. He turns the knob and pushes the door open. He half-turns to me, but the light is off, and I still can't really make out his face. I can tell he has a strong jaw and nose, but seeing so little only makes me long to see more.

"Get some rest. I'm sure it was a long drive." With that, he turns and heads down the stairs, his big body disappearing into the shadows of the cabin.

I go into the room he told me to take and flip on the nearby lamp. I ignore everything but the bed as I toss my bag onto it and let myself fall into its softness.

I'm always alone.

The words run through my mind over and over again. I couldn't catch the tone he was saying them in. Was he alone before I got here, and he liked to be alone? Am I cramping his style? Or was he alone and didn't like it?

I find being alone is bittersweet. It's something I'd wanted for so long, to be able to get lost in myself without my mother clucking all around me. But now the silence is somewhat lonely. It's funny, but that ache didn't start to build until Alex came into my life. Now I'm starting to think he opened a door I'm never going to be able to close.

CHAPTER SIX

alex

I've tossed and turned for the past couple of hours, unable to do much else.

She's here. She's really here.

I hate that I'm a coward and completely unable to talk to her. I froze up the second I laid eyes on her, feeling things I'd never felt. We talked for so long, I felt like I knew her, but I wasn't prepared for seeing her. Nothing could have prepared me for the reality of her beauty.

It's Christmas Eve, and I feel like a kid waiting on Santa Claus to show up. Only Santa Claus is in my guest room upstairs and I'm scared shitless to go up there. If only there was a way to know what she's thinking. Is she disgusted by my scars? Is she disappointed in what she found when she showed up?

God, how I pictured meeting her, seeing a thousand different scenarios in my mind, none of which included her showing up here in the middle of a snowstorm and seeing all my scars.

Sighing, I roll over onto my back and look at the wooden ceiling. I don't know what to do. I need a sign or something. I look over at the fireplace in my bedroom. I watch the burning embers and wish for a Christmas miracle.

Suddenly, there's a pop, and the night light in the bathroom goes out. I sit up, and it's utterly silent. No refrigerator running, no hum of the heat kicking on upstairs. Shit. This is definitely not the Christmas miracle I was referring to.

I get out of bed, go to the bathroom, and flip the switch. Nothing.

There's electric heat and air in the cabin, but in the winter, I often lose power. There's a backup generator, but I never bothered to get kerosene for it. Shit. It's always just been me, and I can make do with the fireplace in the living room and bedroom. Hell, there's a cook stove in the kitchen for me to make hot meals on, and outside is basically a twenty-four-seven refrigerator this time of year. I've never thought twice about the power going out. Until now.

Looking up at the wooden ceiling in my room again, all I can think about is Noelle getting colder by the minute. I start to walk out of my bedroom and realize I need to put some clothes on. Normally, I sleep naked, but I don't think she'd appreciate my showing up in her bedroom naked and asking her to come with me.

My cock twitches at the thought, and I reach down, pinching the tip a little to try to get it to go down. I can't have a fucking hard-on right now.

Taking a few breaths, I look down and see my cock getting bigger instead of softening. "Fuck." Now is not the time. I pull on some tight boxers and some sweats and a long T-shirt. Hopefully, all the layers will cover it up.

I make my way up the stairs and knock lightly guest room door. When there's no answer, I knock a little louder. I pause, waiting, but when there's no sound, I start to panic and wonder if something could have happened to her. Maybe she tried to leave, after all.

Opening the door, I look in and see her sleeping on the bed, still all bundled in her coat. I walk over silently and stand by the bed, looking down at her. The soft moonlight streaming in through the window makes her look like an angel. I never thought in all the times I looked at her picture that she could be more beautiful, but here she is, proving me wrong.

Her soft full lips part slightly, and all I can think about is kissing them.

"*Alex*," she whispers, and I start. I think for a second she's awake and knows I'm here, but she doesn't move and doesn't open her eyes.

She's dreaming of me.

The thought has my heart beating out of my chest, and the biggest, goofiest smile crosses my face. She's dreaming of me. *Me!*

I reach down and scoop her up in my arms, carrying her out of the room. She wakes a little at the movement, wrapping her arms around me, her body clinging to mine.

"Alex?" This time when she says my name, I can hear she's still a little sleepy but coming round.

"The power's gone out, and there's no heat up here. You can sleep downstairs with me." My cock tries to break free of my underwear at the feeling of her in my arms and the image of her in my bed. Even though there are about three feet of layers between me and her body, having her against me is heaven.

The temperature is in single digits outside right now, and the chill is settling in fast upstairs. The house is built well and insulated for the cold, but even a place like this is affected during this kind of winter.

"Okay." She leans into me a little more, and I feel her cheek press against my neck. I nearly lose my footing on the last step. My body goes rigid with equal parts fear and lust.

I walk back to my bedroom and place her on my bed, and she looks up at me sleepily. "Where am I?" She blinks awake, and I turn away from her to grab some more wood and throw it on the hot coals. The fire comes to life, crackling as the flames lick the logs, and I stand still, facing away from Noelle.

"You're in my bed. It will be warm in here for you tonight. I'll sleep on the floor." I grab a blanket and pillow from the closet and throw them on the ground between the bed and the fireplace. "The fire in the living room is out, and it's late." I don't mention that I could get it going again in about sixty seconds, opting instead to keep that fact to myself.

"The bed is huge. You can sleep up here with me.

I'm sure we can manage to stay on our own sides."

My cock aches at the thought of not only having her in my bed but my being in it with her. Her voice once again penetrates my body and makes a chill run down my spine. What I wouldn't give to have her read to me.

I turn to face her, the only light in the room from the fire behind me.

"You should undress." I see her eyes grow wide with shock, and I realize how my words sound. "I mean that you actually stay warmer in cold weather if you're naked. I mean, you should remove your coat and as many clothes as you're comfortable removing. It will help keep you warm tonight in case it gets colder."

I see her nod, and she sits up, removing her heavy coat. I can't help the laugh that escapes me at her Christmas sweater. She looks down at her chest, and I think I can almost see her blush in the weak light.

She reaches under her sweater and I hear a click, and suddenly her sweater lights up. I actually laugh out loud, and I hear her laughter too as the room is illuminated by the blinking lights. "I should have thought of this when you said the power went out." We both laugh a little more as she reaches under again, clicking the switch and turning it off. "Better save that for an emergency."

I love the sound of her giggle, and my own cheeks hurt from smiling. I can't remember the last time I felt so light and…happy.

Trying not to stare as she removes her sweater, I

go around to the other side of the bed, sitting down and facing away from her. I remove my own shirt and slip off my sweatpants, leaving on just my underwear. I'll be fine as long as I stay on my side of the bed. It's a king-size, and I'd have to roll over a couple of times before we touched, so it should be totally okay.

When I'm as undressed as I think I can be, I lie on my back and look up at the ceiling. I feel my heart beating a thousand times a second as I try to breathe regularly. Why does it feel as if I just ran a marathon?

I feel the mattress move, and the top comforter rustles. Oh, God, she's in bed with me. Noelle is in bed with me.

"Thank you, Alex. For everything." I close my eyes as I listen to her words, her voice hypnotizing me. Suddenly, I feel her cool fingers touch my hand and run up my forearm. "I know this isn't what you had planned tonight, but thank you for taking care of me."

"Always," I whisper as I feel her fingers leave my arm, and a silence falls between us.

CHAPTER SEVEN

noelle

I wake plastered to a warm, giant body. It takes me a moment to remember where I am. It all comes flooding back to me, but I stay perfectly still, not wanting to wake Alex. It's still dark out, and I know if he finds out I'm awake I'll have to move, and I'll be so embarrassed. I can't believe how easily I wrapped myself around him.

I guess I'm a cuddler. I've never had the opportunity to find out before if I am or not, but it's pretty freaking clear now with how I'm all over the poor man. Not only did I crash his Christmas, but now I'm taking up his bed and every inch of his personal space.

It's then I realize how truly all over him I am. I have one leg thrown over him, and it's clearly resting on something very large...and very hard. Does that mean he's awake? Do men get boners in their sleep? I try to recall the millions of romances novels I've read and narrated, like they're all factual. I come up blank on the whole boners-when-asleep thing, not having read about it before.

I shuffle a little, making my leg move, and Alex lets out a moaning grunt. I go completely rigid like a dumbass, giving myself away. I wait, but the silence stretches, neither of us calling the other out.

I want to remain still, but my traitorous body takes over, needing to hear that sound again. I shuffle against him again, wanting more of his warmth to seep into me. I feel like burrowing so deep into his heat, I could never get out. I'd never be alone again.

Instantly, I'm on my back. Alex's big body is over mine as he buries his face in my neck. He's so big compared to me, and I'm completely covered beneath him. Fear doesn't hit me at the sudden change in position. A strong dose of lust ripples up my spine and floods my system. It's like nothing I've ever felt before, and I'm immediately addicted.

I lift my hips, needing the contact, letting my legs fall open even more.

"Please. You have to stop." His voice seems strangled and almost pained, but for some reason I can't stop. It's like I no longer have control of my body. Maybe this is what happens when you let yourself go without physical attention for so long. The need for human contact becomes stronger than you can control.

I grip his biceps, my nails digging into his firm

muscles. I just need a little more pressure. It's so close I can feel it. I push my hips up against him, using him for my pleasure. I drag my sex against his, but he remains completely still over me. His hold is firm and steady, and my hips move at just the right angle, and that's all it takes. I explode against him, his name pouring from my lips and filling the silent room. The delicious pleasure cascades through my body as heat spreads between us.

I hold on to him so tightly, as if he'll disappear if I release him. Not wanting to let this moment go, I cling to him. For so long I dreamed of having him over me and now that it's a reality, I can't let it end. The distance he's always tried to keep between us vanishes in this moment, and I'm going to savor it.

When I start to come down, the reality of what I just did hits me. I just rubbed myself against him, using him for my own pleasure. I hear and feel his heavy breathing on top of me, both our bodies gasping for air, filling the silence that seems to hang between us constantly. It's a silence I long to fill with words I can't bring myself to say.

Then he's gone. His warmth leaves my body, taking all of mine with him as he shoots from the bed. The blanket that was covering us hits the floor. The cold air makes goosebumps break out all over my body. He doesn't say a word as he storms from the room, slamming the door behind him so hard I swear I feel the bed shake.

"Holy shit," I whisper to myself. That's when I feel the wetness that's coating the outside of my underwear.

He came.

I thought cumming was a good thing. Clearly Alex isn't happy about it. He stormed from the room like his ass was on fire. Oh, my God. Did I force myself on him? Wait, under him. Can you force yourself under someone?

I roll over, shoving my face into the pillows. Could this get any more awkward? What is wrong with me? Could I have been any clingier? I'm all too happy to crawl into his bed and strip down at his suggestion. A little self-conscious at the time, but that didn't seem to stop me from throwing my clothes off and snuggling deep into his bed. I invited him to join me even after he seemed to want to sleep on the freaking floor.

Clue in, Noelle.

Frustrated, I grab the pillow and throw it across the room. Sitting up, I lean against the headboard and try to think of a way out of this. Maybe I could sneak out in the morning.

This is all so confusing. One minute I felt like he wants to be near me, as if he is longing for me like I am for him. Then the next, it's like having cold water thrown on me.

I remember the sensation of him over me and how it felt so right. The way my hands gripped him tightly, never wanting to let go. The scars under my fingertips. The scars.

It all starts clicking together. He won't look at me. My heart clenches. Does he really think I'm so vain, or do the scars just bother him that much? I haven't seen all of him, but from what I've seen and felt, he's perfect. How he could doubt himself, I have no idea. He is pure male perfection.

I have my flaws, too. My skin may be free of scars, but I carry my own marks. I don't have a perfect hard body like his. I have wide hips and thick thighs. I'm not what you'd call pretty or sexy. Maybe a nerdy kind of cute, but I've often thought I'm a little mousy. Random stretch marks litter my body. They're not scars like his, but they mark me, and I often feel self-conscious about them.

Maybe I could show him it doesn't matter to me. That none of it does. I didn't fall for him because of what he looks like. Hell, I was half in love with him before I ever even saw him. Climbing from the bed, I unhook my bra and drop it to the floor, my panties following suit. I take a deep breath to calm my now-racing heart, and I give myself a pep talk. I can do this. It's all or nothing.

At this point I've got nothing to lose. Either he wants nothing to do with me and I've lost him from my life, or maybe he does want something from me and is too scared to act on it. I can show Alex that I want him by baring myself to him like I want him to do for me.

When I'm standing in front of the door, I give myself one last pep talk. *Stop living in your head, and take what you want.* As I pull the door handle, I come face to face with Alex. He's got both hands braced on the door, and his tall form towers over me.

I gasp at the look on his face.

Hunger, longing, need. It's all there as his eyes roam my naked body before landing back on my face.

The angry-looking scars on the left side of his face run down to his neck. They look like they've healed over time but still look painful.

I reach to touch him, but he's on me instantly. He lifts me into his arms. My feet dangle off the floor as his lips crash onto mine. All the hunger I saw in his eyes bleeds through in his kiss. His tongue pushes into my mouth, taking what it wants. I never knew you could feel so much from a kiss. That it could tell you everything you wanted to know.

He wants me. It's there in the way he's kissing me. He pulls me closer like he's trying to enfold his body in mine. I'm lost in him. I know from this moment on I'll never be the same. I can feel it in every fiber of my body. I'm his.

I feel my back hit the bed, his big body over mine once again. His massive hands come to my face, holding me in place as if he thinks I might try to break away from the kiss. I wrap my arms around him as I kiss him back just as hard, silently showing him I'm not going anywhere. That I'll stay here forever if he asks.

When my hands start to travel over his body, wanting to feel him, he breaks the kiss and buries his face in my neck once again. It's as if he finds it painful for me to rub my hands on him. I won't let him pull away again, so this time I lock my legs around him, my naked body wrapped so tightly around him that if he tries to dart from the room, he'll be taking me with him.

"Look at me."

CHAPTER EIGHTEEN

alex

Closing my eyes tightly, I fight the urge to keep my face buried in her neck. I don't want to look at her, but I can't deny her what she wants.

I look into her beautiful, soft brown eyes, letting her see me. All of me. Her eyes lock with mine, and I wait as they trail down my face and neck. She looks at every mark, then slowly brings her fingertip up to my face, tracing each scar with her gentle touch. Closing my eyes, I breathe in her scent as she explores me.

Having her under my body and rubbing her pussy against my hard cock was my undoing. When I first felt her move earlier, I couldn't control myself and had her pinned beneath me before I thought about what I was doing. I was already on edge when she wrapped her little compact body around me when she was sleeping. It was like the most natural thing in the world for her to do. Then when she rubbed herself to an orgasm on my cock, I came all over her. The tip of my cock peeked out of the waistband of my underwear as she rubbed up and down, exposing some of me. When I felt her heat through my underwear and then the clenches of her orgasm, I pressed the tip of my cock to her panty-covered clit and came with her. The orgasm was fast and unexpected and did nothing to quench my desire for her. It was merely a small drop from the fountain of need I have for her. In fact, it just intensified it.

When I bolted from the room, I immediately regretted leaving her warmth, and turned, gripping the frame of the door to keep myself from going back in. I didn't want to frighten her. Not only with the way I look, but by being some kind of animal and cumming on her like that. But the longer I stood out there, the more I realized that Noelle wanted me. She may not have seen the worst of me, but in her sleep she reached for me. And when she woke up, she still wanted to be near me.

Just as I was about to push the door open, there she stood, completely naked. I didn't stop to think about what I was doing. I just scooped her up and took her back to the bed. I needed her under me, no matter the cost.

As I feel her fingers trail down my chest, I open my eyes to look down at her again. Pressing my hard, underwear-covered cock against her naked pussy, I grind down on her, needing another release.

"Alex," she whispers, rubbing both of her hands

across my chest.

"I have so many things I want to say, Noelle. I don't know where to begin." All these words and emotions are running through me, and I'm all jumbled up. I want to fuck her roughly against every available surface, and then I want to make love to her in all the same places. I want to tell her how much I need her and how addicted I am to her, but I don't want her to reject me. I need to steal this time from her before she finds out how truly gone I am for her and leaves this cabin.

"Make love to me, Alex. Please." Her eyes meet mine, and I can see need in them. I see something else, too, but I don't know what it is. Lust? Something stronger?

"I...Noelle."

"Don't make me beg." She laughs a little, running her hands through my hair and then down my face. Suddenly, she sobers a little, holding me tighter. "I've never done this before, but I need you, Alex. I feel it deep in my soul. I need you inside me."

Fuck.

Her words shouldn't break me in two, but they do. Knowing that she wants part of me inside her body, taking her first. I'll be the last, too, if I have anything to say about it. Maybe I could chain her to me. Leave something of me inside her so she'll never be free of me.

Leaning down, I take her lips in a passionate kiss, telling her with my body what I can't say in words. I kiss down her chin and neck, licking the dip at her collarbone and running my teeth along the sensitive skin there. I feel her shudder under me as I move down, licking each of her nipples and biting the flesh of her breasts. My big hands squeeze them together, loving each one equally.

Noelle's moans fill the room, and I shiver at her voice. It's so erotic and sensual. It's as if all the fantasies I've ever had of her reading to me have come to life.

"Talk to me, Noelle. Tell me all the things you want me to do to you. I'm addicted to your voice."

As I lick down her stomach, still pinching her nipples as I move lower, she starts to tell me what she wants.

"Please, Alex. I need you between my thighs and licking my pussy. Don't tease me. I'm so close to cumming just having you on top of me."

Once again the sound of her voice soothes me and makes me impossibly hard. I move down between her legs, shouldering apart her thighs and making room for my broad body.

Pressing my face to her pussy, I inhale her sweetness. Her lower lips, already sticky from her earlier orgasm, dampen with need. I stick my tongue out and flatten it against her clit, giving her long thick licks. Her moans grow louder and louder as I taste her nectar, the flavor coating my tongue and intensifying my addiction. I growl against her pussy, thinking about how it's untouched and how she wants me to be the one to take it for the first time.

I have no clue how someone so perfect is untouched. How has no one taken her as their own yet? I'll lock her in my cabin and keep her forever.

Moving down just a little, I stick my tongue inside her, feeling a tight squeeze from her needy pussy.

"Baby, I don't know if I'll fit," I say, kissing the inside of her thigh and moving back up to suck on her clit.

"Fuck!" she shouts, as the suction on her clit makes her back bow off the bed. "I'll make it. I need you, Alex. Please."

Biting down just a little on her clit, I flick my tongue across it a few times before I feel her start to tense up. Just as she's about to orgasm, I press two thick fingers inside her pussy. I rub the sweet spot just inside her, and it only takes two strokes before she's cumming on my fingers and in my mouth.

She reaches down, fisting my hair and screaming loudly as the fierce orgasm flows through her body. Her pussy clamps down on my fingers, but I don't move, still rubbing and sucking her off.

The taste of her orgasm is even sweeter than how she tasted before she came, and my cock leaks cum in response. He wants to have that sweetness coating him.

Once I've wrung the last of her orgasm from her, I give her sweet clit one last kiss and move up her body. I push down my underwear as I go, kicking it off, wanting to be naked with her. As I line my bare cock with her opening, it occurs to me that as she's a virgin she probably isn't protected.

I grab the base of my cock and hold myself there as I look into her eyes. She's got a slight sheen of sweat across her forehead, and her cheeks are flushed from her powerful orgasm.

"I want you raw, Noelle. Nothing between us. I'll take care of you if I get you pregnant, but I won't wear a condom with you. Not ever." She looks into my eyes, and after a second she licks her lips and nods. "I've never ridden bareback before, but I won't have anything between us." She nods again. I know I'm clean. I haven't been with anyone in years. I didn't even have a desire to after the first time I heard Noelle's voice. From that moment I knew another wouldn't do. I thought I could never have her and was planning to be celibate for the rest of my life because I knew I'd never want another.

I lean down slightly so she doesn't miss what I'm about to say. "I won't pull out either. Once I get inside you, I'm cumming in you."

Her breath catches, but once again she nods. I feel her lift her hips in invitation, and all I can hope is that my seed clings to her womb and I bind us together forever.

I press my cock to her opening, and at the first touch of her heat, I thrust in hard, breaking through her virginity in one movement. I didn't want to cause her prolonged pain, so I thought popping her cherry in one thrust would be best.

Feeling her tense under me, I wonder if I did the right thing. I brace my elbows on either side of her head, rubbing her forehead and trying to soothe her with kisses. After a moment, the pain seems to ease, and she starts to clench around me.

Her pussy is tighter than anything I've ever felt, and it's squeezing me almost to the point of pain. I have to grit my teeth and fight myself not to cum, not wanting to end this too soon.

I start to make small shallow thrusts, working my way up to fully moving in and pulling out. After a few more strokes, Noelle is moaning and scratching at my back, begging me to go harder. I bury my face in her neck and give her what she wants, all the while trying not to cum too soon.

I feel her legs go around my waist, her heels digging into my ass. I moan at the feeling of being inside her tight body. The sound of our sexes slapping the sticky passion between us is loud in the quiet room.

"Oh, God, Noelle." I take her mouth again in a kiss like no other, trying to make her feel what I feel.

Her pussy clamps down on me one final time as her body explodes in an orgasm. I swallow her cries, wanting to devour her passion, as I thrust into her and release my own orgasm. I feel the cum pump out of me as her pussy squeezes it from my cock. My seed coats her unprotected womb, possibly making a baby to bind her to me.

The thought has me pumping even more cum into her, wanting her to be mine in every way.

Once we've both come down from our peaks, I kiss her lips softly and smile down at her. I feel like I'm floating, and at the same time I'm completely spent.

Not wanting to pull out of her, I roll us over so my big body isn't crushing hers. She lies across my chest, and I play with her hair, whispering all the ways I'm going to love her body tonight.

CHAPTER NINE

noelle

"That was…" I trail off, searching for the words for what that was. My body feels like Jell-O, and I have no desire to leave this spot for the rest of my life. His cock is still nestled deep inside me, as hard as he was when he first entered.

"Perfection," Alex finishes for me, drawing my eyes up to his. I see a fire dancing in the deep blue depths. 'Perfection' works, but it was more than that. All of this feels…life-changing. He holds my stare this time, not looking away as he gives me a clear view of his face. The fire lends a glow to the room, letting me see all of what he's been trying to hide.

I don't want to hide. I'm sick of this game. Just like when I got naked and went after him, I'm going to throw my cards on the table. All or nothing. I can't go back to what we had before. Not even just working for him, but being forced to have daily calls with him and not being with him would rip me in two. There's no going back. I'll just fling myself over the cliff and I pray he's going to catch me.

"I've wanted this for so long." His eyes widen a little at my words like he's shocked by them. How he doesn't get it, I have no freaking idea. Any red-blooded woman would want him. He's beautiful in a rough manly kind of way. His scars only add to his whole appeal. After all the romance novels I've read, I seem to have found my own sweet, brooding, scared hero. I want to keep him, and I want him to want to keep me, too.

He said things when we were making love. How much of that was heat of the moment babbling, and how much was real?

"I've wanted you since the first time heard your voice. Before you ever even knew I existed," he admits. The words he said to me when we were making love ring through my mind. "*Talk to me, Noelle. Tell me all the things you want me to do to you. I'm addicted to your voice.*"

"You're addicted to my voice?"

He huffs out a laugh. "Yeah." He rolls us both so I'm pinned under him again. "Your voice is where it started. Now I think I'm addicted to every part of you. Your eyes, your lips, your innocence, your body and the way you can talk to me for hours on end and just let me listen. The way you get comfortable in silence and the way your breath does this little hitch every time you do a narration and the hero says 'I love you.' All of it. Every part of it. I could go on for days."

"But you…" I search my brain, trying to put everything together. So much of this has seemed one-sided for so long. "I didn't think you wanted me."

"Does this feel like I don't want you?" His cock slides out of me a little and thrusts back in.

"You're a man. The wind makes you hard," I tease, wiggling my hips, wanting him to do that again.

"I hadn't gotten hard since the accident until I heard your voice. Now I can't seem to get *un*-hard." The smile on his face lets me know that this doesn't seem to bother him in the least.

That shouldn't make me happy, but it does. That I have some special power—that only I can get him off—pleases me.

"What happened?" I reach up and touch one of his scars, and he leans into my palm, craving the feel of me.

"Wrong place, wrong time. Got hit by a car."

"Oh, God." Horror fills my voice, but he brushes his thumb across my cheek, soothing me.

"I'm fine. It happened years ago," he says, his voice devoid of emotion.

"Is that why you're all the way out here in the middle of almost nowhere?" I know his company is pretty big and he has a few other people working for him. I have to deal with them from time to time.

"At first, yeah. It's kind of grown on me now. Life's not so busy. I like the quiet a lot more than I thought I would."

I know the feeling. I've always been a homebody.

I just stay in the town so I can have some human contact from time to time. I know if I lived out in a beautiful cabin like this, I'd probably never see another soul until my mom came and dragged me from it kicking and screaming.

"Don't you get lonely?"

"I was at first. Then I found you."

"Liar, you hardly talk to me." I playfully smack his arm.

"I don't talk much because I want to hear you. If I'm talking, you're not."

"But I like hearing you, too."

"Then I'll talk until I can't utter another word if it makes you happy. As long as you stay here with me."

"You want me to stay here with you? Like, for the holiday?" My heartbeat picks up as I wonder what he'll say.

"Yeah for the holiday." He pauses for a second, and I see what looks like uncertainty creep into his eyes. "And after."

"After?" I push, wanting more. It's hanging in front of me, so close I can almost grab it. I want his words and for him to ask me to stay.

"Forever," he finally says, and I can tell he's worried what I might say. My chest fills with warmth, but it feels too good to be true.

"Is it too soon?" I know it's a stupid question. Hell, we just had unprotected sex. Our baby could be growing inside me as we speak, but I need him to give me more. He's hiding so much of himself from me. I want to know we're on the same page, that he's just as crazy about me as I am about him.

"I'll make you so fucking happy, Noelle. I know you're perfect for me. I've listened to you talk for hours on end. You're it for me. I know it to my core, and I'll spend every day showing you that I'm it for you. That we belong together."

"Why aren't you using the audios I made?" The question has been hanging in my mind, and after all the sweet things he's said to me, this one thing is still not adding up. He liked my voice so much, and he used me for so many jobs…

He blushes at my question like he's embarrassed.

"I-I…*shit*." He brushes a few strands of hair out of my face. "I didn't like the idea of others hearing you say all the sex stuff in the audios. I wanted it to just be mine."

"You kept them for yourself?" He must have a stockpile of my audios hidden away. I don't know why, but it is adorably cute. I wonder what he does with them. I'll have to ask him later, for sure.

"God, this makes me sound crazy, but yeah, I kept them for myself. Seems I do a lot of things I shouldn't when it comes to you." He says it like he has a few more secrets he's keeping, and I want them. If we're doing this, jumping into this so quickly, then I need to know it all.

"Are there more things I should know?" It should be freaking me out, but thinking that he's been stalkerish makes me feel warm inside. Like he's got all these little dirty secrets about me just for himself.

His grip tightens on me like I might try to get away from him. "I ran a check on you when I first found you. Learned everything I could. I also might have hired someone to watch you for me."

"You have someone watching me?" Now that I can't believe. Watching me would have to be the world's most boring job. I maybe leave the house once a week, and that's just to go to the store. I get everything pretty much just shipped right to my front door.

"I was worried someone would steal you," he says with such certainly. He says it like it's a real possibility that someone is really going to come and take me away.

"Steal me?" I don't even know what to do with that.

"Yeah. If I had met you, I would've scooped you up and never let another man near you. I got scared you'd meet someone and then…" His words trail off. He doesn't even want to finish the sentence. I can see the uncertainly in his face. He's scared I'm going to run from him now that I know the truth. But the grip he has on me won't let me go anywhere, even if I wanted to.

Nope. He'll never be rid of me now.

CHAPTER TEN

alex

"I don't want you to ever leave me, Noelle. I can't bear the thought of not having you for even a second now that I've got you under me."

She smiles so big and brightly at me, it's as if she can feel the same things I've always felt for her.

"This is insane," she tells me, leaning up to kiss me quickly. "I feel this pull between us, and I've never felt anything like this before. It's…it's—"

"Love," I finish for her.

"Love," she repeats, and we stare into each other's eyes.

Thrusting into Noelle gently, I try to take her tenderly this time. Less hurried and less afraid of the moment vanishing.

I kiss her passionately and whisper my promises

of devotion and desire. And when we find our peaks together, her name on my lips and mine on hers, I cradle her in my arms and hold her while she sleeps, truly happy, inside and out, for the first time in my life.

———————•—•———————

I reach for her every hour throughout the night, making love multiple times until exhaustion carries us off to sleep. Most of the time, I wake up still inside her, one round of passion leading into another.

Her sex has to be sore, but she keeps clinging to me just as much as I've clung to her. Neither of us want to separate.

When the first touch of sunlight comes through the windows, I kiss her shoulder and nuzzle her neck. "Merry Christmas, Noelle."

Smiling, she turns in my arms to face me, kissing my neck and burrowing deeper into me. "Merry Christmas, Alex."

"I have a present for you."

Noelle sits up a little and looks at me. Her hair's a mess and she's still half-asleep, but she perks up at the word 'present.'

"You got me a Christmas present? How did you even know I would come here?"

"I didn't know. I got it for you and I thought I would send it to you, but I chickened out. Then I thought maybe I would save it for your birthday." I blush a little, feeling silly for the idea, but Noelle beams at me, leaning up and kissing my cheek.

I turn to get out of bed, not wanting to leave her warmth but wanting to keep that smile on her face, and I feel a sharp sting across my ass.

"Ouch. Did you just spank me?"

Turning around, I see her sitting up in bed with the covers around her waist, her full breasts on display. A mischievous look is on her face, and she just nods at me.

"Oh, turnabout is fair play, baby." I dive back on the bed, and we giggle as I wrestle her over and give her three spanks on her bottom. Her squeals of surprise turn into moans as I lean down and kiss where my hand just made a faint pink mark. "Do you want more, or do you want your present?"

"Both," she says into the pillow, and I bite her ass cheek, giving her what she's asking for.

I climb on top of her as she remains face down on the bed. Spreading her legs just slightly, I press my cock to her opening from behind, her entrance tighter than normal in this position, and I have to work my way inside her.

She raises her ass, giving me access to all of her, and I slide in easily. Once I'm fully seated inside her tight channel, I lay most of my weight on top of her and start to thrust. Long deep strokes make the angle delicious for her, and she moans louder and louder.

My cock is still hard as a rock even after all our rounds of passion, and I'm ready to cum in her again. I don't know if I'll ever get enough of her.

I work to rub her sweet spot inside, making sure that every stroke is giving her the most pleasure possible, and she's soon clenching around me. I kiss her neck and nibble her shoulder, and her over-sensitized skin responds.

She clutches the sheets beneath her and screams out her orgasm as I bottom out inside her. Once again I fill up her unprotected womb, letting my seed spill inside her. Noelle's overflowing with it at this point, and there's no doubt in my mind I've put my baby inside her.

Once her twitches have finally stopped, I pull from her body and turn her over. I kiss each nipple before moving down her belly and kissing her clit. Once I've tenderly kissed her sweet places, I stand up and go to the living room, grabbing her present from under the tree.

I come back to find her still in the same spot with a giant smile on her face. I laugh as I sit on the bed beside her and hold out the small box.

Sitting up, she takes it from me, her eyes twinkling with excitement as she opens it up. After she's got the paper off, she opens the long skinny box and pulls out the chain.

"What is it?" she asks, holding the gold necklace in her hand.

"It's your voice, actually." When she looks at me questioningly, I point to the waves that run along the middle of the chain. "I listened to your recordings so many times, I think I have them memorized, so I took a couple of words and had the sound waves shaped in gold. The three small sections of lines show the words that I loved hearing from you the most."

She looks at me with unshed tears in her eyes. "What does it say?"

"I love you."

She throws herself into my arms, clinging to me. I cling to her just as fiercely, wanting her to know that what I say is true.

"I love you, too, Alex."

I hold her close, kissing her and wiping away her tears. "I have loved you from the moment I heard your voice. Thank you for coming here, and being my Christmas miracle."

EPILOGUE

noelle

Christmas Eve, five years later.

"But what if the power goes out?" Nicholas asks, a little fear in his eyes.

"Your dad is the greatest woodsman who ever lived. He won't let anything happen to us. Besides, if the power goes out then we get to have Christmas dinner over the fire. It's kind of fun." His eyes brighten at the idea, and I kiss his forehead, tucking him into bed. "Goodnight, my love. Get some sleep. Santa will be here soon enough."

"Goodnight, Mommy. I love you."

"I love you, too."

I close the door to his room and make my way downstairs. I find Alex in our bedroom, pulling out the train set 'Santa' got Nicholas for Christmas.

"Is he asleep?"

"Not even close. Better wait a bit before we set that out. Just in case."

Alex puts the toy down, walking over to me with a seductive look in his eyes. "Hmm. I wonder what we could do while we wait. What could we possibly do with all this free time on our hands?"

I giggle and melt into him, loving the feel of him against me. We've been living here in our cabin for the past five years, and each day together is better than the last. I'm still head over heels madly in love with my husband, and if the way he can't keep his hands off me is any indication, he feels the same.

We had our little boy, Nicholas, nine months exactly after our first Christmas together, and we decided to wait a while and see if we wanted any more. Alex and I are simple people and didn't want a large family. A few years went by after having our son, and we agreed that our trio was perfect.

"I thought you were going to make me s'mores?" I moan as Alex's tongue meets my collarbone.

"Tell you what. You let me eat your pussy, and then I'll make you s'mores."

"It's like you're not even trying to win anything here," I laugh as I let him unbutton my jeans.

"Baby, I've got you. I've already won everything."

My laugh turns into another moan as Alex kneels down in front of me, kissing me in all the right places.

He's so good to me, I can't believe it sometimes. Maybe I'll read him that new Ruby Dixon book, Ice Planet Holiday, out loud tonight. He's been waiting for the latest Barbarian story, and he loves it when I get to the sex scenes.

I close my eyes and smile, thinking this might be our best Christmas yet.

OTHER TITLES BY ALEXA RILEY

CURVY

GUARDING HIS OBSESSION

RIDING RED

MECHANIC

COACH

THE VIRGIN DUET

THEIR STEPSISTER

MY NEW STEP-DAD

P.S.... YOU'RE MINE

OWNING HER INNOCENCE

OWNING THE BEAST

TAKING THE FALL SERIES

FORCED SUBMISSION SERIES

MISTRESS AUCTIONS SERIES

GHOST RIDERS SERIES

89658373R00110

Made in the USA
Lexington, KY
01 June 2018